Also by Natasha D. Fraz

Devotionals

The Life Your Spirit Craves

Not Without You

Not Without You Prayer Journal

The Life Your Spirit Craves for Mommies

Pursuit

Fiction

Love, Lies & Consequences

Through Thick & Thin: Love, Lies & Consequences Book 2

Shattered Vows: Love, Lies & Consequences Book 3

Out of the Shadows: Love, Lies & Consequences Book 4

Kairos: The Perfect Time for Love

Fate (The Perfect Time for Love series)

With Every Breath (The McCall Family Series, book 1)

With Every Step (The McCall Family Series, book 2)

With Every Moment (The McCall Family Series, book 3)

The Reunion (Langston Sisters, book 1)

The Wrong Seat (Langston Sisters, book 2)

Non-Fiction
How Long Are You Going to Wait?

Published by Encouraging Works
Printed by Lightning Source, Inc.

ISBN: 979-89895509-0-6

Printed in the United States of America

Editor: Chandra Sparks Splond

For autographed copies, please visit:
www.natashafrazier.com

Acknowledgements

Here we are again. 😊 Another story in the books! The Langston Sisters series is now complete. But don't worry, we'll see more of them in the Four Kings series, I think. I've enjoyed writing Layla and Mason's story and, as always, I hope that you'll enjoy it as much as me.

None of this would be possible if my Heavenly Father didn't give me the capacity and provision to do the thing that I love—write. So, thank You, Lord.

My husband, Eddie, and my children Eden, Ethan, and Emilyn—thank you for your love and support. I couldn't do any of this without you all sacrificing a moment or two with me every now and then.

My sister, Amber—Thank you for stepping in to help with my children when needed and often without being asked. My sister, Courtney—thank you for your encouragement and spreading the word! 😊

Chandra—Thank you for your editing expertise. This story wouldn't be as amazing without you.

Special thank you to my sisters, Tiera, Toccara, and Shenitra, who have prayed with me and encouraged me in my journey.

Page 35— I am thankful for your encouragement and feedback throughout my writing process. Thank you for making me better.

Mom and Dad—I wouldn't be here if it weren't for you. Thank you for encouraging me to "go for the trophy."

My CBLR family—Thank you for your support, readership, and love. I appreciate each of you.

And the Dream Team—Thank you for listening, providing feedback, and brainstorming with me. Teamwork certainly makes the dream work. Thank you for being part of my team.

Dearest reader—Thank you for supporting me by reading, reviewing, and sharing my books with others. (Please don't stop.) You're all I think about as I write. Enjoy Layla and Mason's story.

Natasha

THE
MISSING LINK

Langston Sisters Series Book 3

CHAPTER ONE

*T**rapped inside of a dark, tight, claustrophobic space, Layla Langston couldn't breathe. She couldn't be sure how long she'd been stuffed inside of the box, but her oxygen level was on its last leg. Her breathing grew heavier, and the space grew warmer and stuffier. A mix of pinewood, her cocoa-scented body cream, and sweat permeated the tiny area. She fanned her fingers to feel around the tight space, but she couldn't move her hand away from her side. Layla attempted a squeal, but the sound from her lips was muffled. She hardly recognized her own voice.*

Lord, what is happening to me?

A lone tear rolled down her cheek—or at least she expected to feel the dampness on her face. Instead, the tear soaked what she was certain to be some sort of mummy wrappings. Her breathing became labored and more ragged. Every struggled rise of her chest collided with the pinewood of the box. Someone may as well have had their fingers wrapped around her throat.

Don't panic and lose the rest of your oxygen. You're smart. You can figure your way out of this.

Layla squeezed her eyes tight. This had to be a dream. If she squeezed tight and long enough, and counted down from ten, maybe she'd wake up.

Ten, nine, eight, seven, six, five, four, three, two, one.

She opened her eyes, pushed out a stream of air, and canvased her surroundings. Fresh, clean air. White curtains and a matching duvet cover, bedroom furniture fit for royalty, and a room filled with blessed light comforted her. She was still in Nassau for her sister Ava's wedding.

It had only been a dream.

The fifth one this week. Each time she had the dream, the visions became more daunting. More frightening. More real. There had to be something she was missing, right? Hadn't she always warned her sisters to pay attention to the dreams she had? Only she couldn't be certain how to take heed to her own messages because she didn't know what the dreams—nightmares—meant.

Layla tossed the luxury covers to the side, climbed out of bed, and donned her matching silk bridesmaid robe. She sauntered down the open wood staircase into the kitchen of their Langston beach home to brew a carafe of coffee, but found her sisters, Crystal and Ava, already gathered around the breakfast table laughing and chatting. The rays of sunlight bounced off the cool blue pool water and filtered through the kitchen window, shining on the two of them as if was a congratulatory message from God Himself.

Layla leaned in and hugged Crystal first, her protruding belly making it impossible for her to sit close to the table.

"Morning."

"Morning to you, too. Thought we'd have to knock the door down to wake you up. You're wasting precious time. We have to enjoy this beautiful island."

Layla smiled and shrugged. "Yeah, I know. Needed the rest, I guess."

This morning would be a rare occasion where she wouldn't mention her dreams to either of her sisters. Today should be festive and light, not stomach-wrenching and gloomy based on what her sleeping thoughts revealed.

Layla turned her attention to Ava. "How are you feeling? Cold feet yet?"

Crystal laughed. "You know her feet have been on fire since the moment she met Zack."

Layla snorted. "Right. I must have forgotten who I'm talking about. A better question would be, can you wait another few hours?"

"Hush, both of you. I've waited all this time. A few more hours couldn't hurt. It's almost surreal though. I just hope I'm ready to be his wife."

Crystal cocked her head to the side. "You're ready alright. There are at least two simple things to remember, and you'll be all good."

Layla poured her coffee and took her seat at the table, scooting close as if Crystal were about to reveal some big secret. "What's that?" she asked as if she was the one about to get married and in need of advice.

Crystal smirked and hiked an eyebrow. "Respect him and love him."

"I respect and love him already."

Crystal rubbed her belly. "I mean, love him regularly—as regularly as possible."

Ava shimmied her shoulders. "Not a problem. Can't wait to do that anyway."

Layla and Crystal laughed.

Layla shrugged one shoulder and sipped her coffee. "I guess I'll just tuck that info away in the back of my mind for when I need it. Even if I forget, I'm sure you two will remind me. By that time, Crystal will probably have a whole basketball team."

"Slow your roll, sis. Maybe one more, that's it. This kid is wearing me out already."

Layla reached over and rubbed Crystal's belly. "Hang in there, Marcel, Jr. Don't do my sister too bad."

"Listen to your aunt because she'll be doing plenty of babysitting."

"You can count on it, but while we have this moment, let's toast to Ava and Zack." Layla raised her mug in the air. "Ava, I'm proud of the woman you've become, and I wish you and Zack nothing but peace, love, and happiness. You both deserve it. I've watched the way he looks at you, treats you, and adores you. I think I speak for the family when I say my heart is at ease knowing that you'll have him as your husband. To sixty-plus years of bliss."

Ava laughed. "Thanks, but did you have to add the number of years?"

Layla shrugged. "Hey, I said plus."

Crystal laughed and cleared her throat. She raised her mug of hot tea. "Okay. My turn. If you ask me, Zack wanted you the moment he carried you into the hospital, but what I love most is you love him equally as much as he loves you. Hold on to each other. Keep God as the cornerstone of your marriage, and you two will be able to handle whatever life brings your way. Cheers."

"Cheers," both Ava and Layla said with their mugs lifted in the air.

As happy as Layla was for Crystal's and Ava's new journeys, uncertainty mixed with excitement filled her about her own. Up until this second, work at Langston Brands and family defined her life, but the time now came for her to prioritize her own happiness. With Crystal, a soon-to-be new mother, and Ava, a new wife, Layla knew her moment had come to seek her own adventure. She loved her family and the business they'd built, but she didn't want to marry Langston Brands, and she didn't have plans to be the third wheel in either of their relationships.

She sipped her hot coffee—coffee that seemed to pool in the bottom of her belly with each sip. Images of being stuffed in the pinewood box filled her thoughts.

"Okay, Crys won't mention it, but I will. Forget about me and Zack for a moment. What's going on with you, Lay? Are you seriously going to leave the business? And are we really going to sit here and act like you leaving won't affect us?"

Layla should have known her sisters wouldn't keep quiet about her resignation letter. While they assured her they supported her decision, this confrontation couldn't be avoided.

5

"Ava, like I said two weeks ago, I have to do this for me. You both are getting everything you wanted. Do I have to be the exception?"

Ava seemed to relax in her seat and consider Layla's side, while Crystal, on the other hand, wasn't quite convinced.

"Is this about Ava getting married?"

Layla massaged her temple. "No, Crys. It's about me pursuing something for myself for a change. I need you both to support me like you said you would."

Ava reached across the table and covered Layla's hand with hers. "We do support you. We just want you to be sure this is the right move and you're not making a hasty decision."

"I've wanted a career in journalism for a long time, and now that I have the opportunity, I have to take it. I'm not leaving our family, just changing careers."

Crystal's features softened, and understanding filled her eyes. "We know you're not leaving us. It just feels like you are."

"I think that baby has you overly emotional. Everything will be fine. Plus, if it doesn't work out, I'm coming back for my job."

Crystal laughed. "In that case, I'll hold it for you until I return from maternity leave."

"Fair enough."

Could the career change be what her dream referred to? Before today, Layla hadn't assessed her feelings about the new lives her sisters were about to embark on nor her interview for the journalist position with *The Houston Exposure*. Perhaps her subconscious whispered her truth—at forty years old, she felt stuck.

And she'd do whatever she had to do to get unstuck, even if it meant stepping away for a while.

Away from Langston Brands.

Away from her family.

Away from everything she'd ever known so she could find and embrace the journey that was hers to take.

∞

Nothing brought Mason Sterling satisfaction quite like exposing the story behind the story. And his latest article in *The Houston Exposure* about one of Houston's most prominent oncologists intentionally misdiagnosing patients to commit insurance fraud would likely win him the Pulitzer Prize. While great, he didn't do his job well to win awards, but he did it to satisfy his curiosity and write excellent articles that exposed the wrongdoing taking place in his city. There was no way Dr. Wang should be allowed to practice medicine and tout herself as an oncologist with a ninety-percent success rate in curing cancer patients. Her stats were high because many of her patients never had cancer to begin with.

Gathered inside of The Majestic Metro in downtown Houston, Mason stood in the front row of the crowd and watched as his father, Walter Sterling, addressed his constituents from center stage. He couldn't be prouder of him pursuing his dreams to bring change to the city of Houston and the nation. Some of Houston's top business owners, politicians, and friends were in the building. Marcel Singleton, Houston's district attorney, was also among the crowd. He lifted his glass of champagne in salute and strode toward Mason.

"You're pretty strong with your pen. Is your father paving the way for a political future for you, Mr. Sterling?"

"You don't have to be formal with me, attorney." Mason sipped his bottled water. "Politics is not my calling. This is his dream, not mine."

The crowd erupted into applause and whistles. Mason and Marcel joined them.

When the applauding subsided, Marcel said, "You never know what the future holds. Keep your options open. I've read your articles in *The Houston Exposure*. You seem to have an affinity for change and accountability."

"Yeah, but there are different ways to handle it. Not everyone is made for politics."

"I get it. No pressure here." Marcel fist bumped Mason. "I've got to run, though. My wife is near the end of her pregnancy, and I don't want to be away from her for too long. Give your pops my well wishes."

"Will do, and congratulations."

"Thanks, man. Appreciate it."

When Marcel walked away, Mason entertained a few other guests while he waited for his father to shake hands and answer questions. Watching him work the room in his three-piece suit, Mason couldn't understand why he hadn't taken the leap into politics years ago. He appeared to be in his element, a natural. The crowd loved him too—hung on to his every word like birds who'd just captured a worm—but ultimately, he understood why his father waited until now.

When Mason's mother died, his father insulated himself. For three years, life stopped for Walter Sterling because Stephanie Sterling was Mason's and his father's world. It had been difficult for them both to move on. And now that his father had taken the leap to pursue his dreams, Mason couldn't be prouder.

After he'd made his rounds, his father walked over to him, placed one hand on his shoulder, and enclosed Mason's hand with the other. "How are you, tonight? Too much for you yet?"

Mason chuckled. "You know I go with the flow. I'm here for you, so whatever you need, I've got you."

"Spoken like a true—"

Mason interrupted. "Don't even say it. You know this is not the kind of life I want."

His father nodded with an I-don't-believe-you-but-I-will-drop-the-issue-for-now smirk.

Mason's father hinted at the idea of him running for office alongside him, but Mason had never been interested in politics, other than to expose the wrongdoings of politicians. As far as he was concerned, an investigative journalist was the perfect career for him, and he had no plans of doing anything else. Why would he give up the opportunity to satisfy his curiosity regularly and write about it?

Two men, also dressed in suits, approached them.

"Son, I'd like to introduce you to two of my biggest supporters, Donovan Finch and Chuck Williams."

Mason shook both of their hands. "Nice to meet you both." He engaged in small talk with his father, Donovan, and Chuck for a few minutes before they left the group. Chuck mentioned he was going home, and Donovan worked the room like he was running for office.

Mason flipped his wrist to check the time. "Still up for dinner at Perry's, or are you too worn out, old man?"

"I'll never turn down a free steak."

Mason chuckled. "Smooth way of letting me know that I'm covering the check." Mason clapped his father's shoulder. "I'll see you there."

"I'm right behind you after I shake a few more hands."

He left his father's side to take the thirty-minute drive to Perry's Steakhouse & Grille, the restaurant they'd frequented after every political event to celebrate his father's progress. It was Mason's way of showing his father how proud he was of him. And this evening wasn't any different. With his radio tuned to Houston's R&B station, he cruised along Highway 59 to the restaurant. His chest filled with pride when the deejay mentioned his father's rally and encouraged listeners to vote in the upcoming election.

By the time he parked, he was tired of listening to the songs playing. He lifted his hand to switch from the radio to his Bluetooth, but stopped when the deejay interrupted the current song to announce breaking news.

"I've just received some unfortunate news. There's been an explosion downtown near Congressman Hopeful Walter Sterling's political rally. My sources cannot confirm whether there were any casualties. Please say a prayer. I'll be back on when I know more."

The air constricted in Mason's chest. Knowing his father, he probably hadn't even left The Majestic Metro yet. "Siri, call Dad."

His father didn't pick up the phone, which was odd because even in the middle of a conversation, he would typically answer to say he would call him back.

Something was wrong. He could feel it in his bones.

Mason called again. This time the line opened. He released a heavy sigh. Worry had almost overtaken him for a moment.

"Hello?"

A woman's voice answered his father's phone. "Hello, Mason." She sounded like she'd been running. "Where are you? There's been an explosion…Your father was injured…he's been taken to St. Luke's."

He didn't ask any questions. All he could think about was how he could cut his drive time in half to get to St. Luke's Hospital. He shifted his truck into gear and sped out of the restaurant's parking lot. So many thoughts plundered through his mind. If he'd stayed and waited with his father, would he have been able to get him out of harm's way? What caused the explosion? And would his father live through this?

Mason whispered a prayer. *Lord, please let my dad make it.*

After cutting off several vehicles along the way and breaking every traffic law created, he screeched to a halt near the hospital's emergency entrance. He didn't even take the time to find a proper parking space.

He jumped out and ran through the automatic doors where he didn't stop until he reached the sign-in desk.

"Walter Sterling. Did they bring him here? That's my father." He fought to keep a controlled voice to no avail. His booming voice rattled the nurse behind the desk. Her shoulders shook and her eyes bucked.

She lifted the phone receiver and kept her eyes on him. Her voice was low while she spoke, and her face showed no emotion.

"The doctor will be out to see you in a moment."

Mason paced the vinyl flooring for far too many minutes. He'd never understood why hospitals even had emergency rooms because he'd never seen anyone acting with enough urgency—and his father being injured was an urgent matter.

Mason approached the nurse again. "Ma'am, I'm here to see Walter Sterling. Where's the doctor?"

Another nurse walked into the area, and the desk nurse seemed relieved. She approached Mason. "May I have your name?"

"Mason Sterling. Walter Sterling is my father. I need to see him."

She tapped the screen on an electronic tablet. "The doctor will be out to see you shortly. Please follow me."

The nurse led him to a more private area and disappeared. How many more times did he have to hear the doctor would be out before he actually saw him or her?

Mason huffed and paced for another twenty minutes in the small space. He stopped short when an older Black woman wearing a white coat entered the room. When they locked eyes, his feet couldn't move fast enough to get to her.

"I'm Mason Sterling. Is my father okay? When can I see him?"

He searched her eyes for any sign of his father's health status, but her face was as emotionless as the nurse who led him into the room minutes ago.

"Hi, Mason. I'm Dr. Riley." She gestured toward a nearby chair. "Please have a seat."

"I'd rather stand. When can I see him?"

"I'm sorry, Mason. Your father didn't make it."

Mason stood paralyzed.

Unable to move.

Unable to speak.

Unable to think.

She continued talking, but the words tumbled out of her mouth like puzzle pieces of the same color. He couldn't decipher a single word. Blood rushed to his brain. His heart raced fast enough for him to believe he'd need a hospital bed.

A knot formed in Mason's throat that he couldn't swallow. If he did, tears would overtake him. Pain settled there. His stomach taut. All of his muscles tightened.

Mason belted out, "No." Air barely escaped his lungs as he had to force himself to breathe.

The pain in his chest was just as real physically as it was emotionally. His heart ripped into pieces. That was the only explanation for the stabbing sensation in his chest. His eyes stung as tears spilled down his cheeks soaking his collar.

He finally sat in that chair Dr. Riley suggested he take. She'd mentioned something about whether there was someone else she could call for him. Usually, his father would be that person, and now he had no one.

CHAPTER TWO

Two-and-half months had gone by—seventy-five days since the explosion that ultimately led to his father's death. No one at fault. No satisfactory answers.

Too many negatives in his opinion.

He'd just finished his first assignment since his father's passing, exposing corporate fraud among a local retail chain. Typically, at the end of an assignment, he'd talk about his findings with his father when he submitted his article to his boss and friend, Simon Taylor, but that explosion took that option away from him. This was his new life—a life without his father.

Now, the closest person to him was Simon. He invited Mason out to Biggio's, a local sports bar, to watch the Houston Rockets play against the Dallas Mavericks. They talked about random topics, which led Mason to believe Simon only wanted to get him out of the house. Too much time alone couldn't be good for anyone, including Mason, the ultimate loner. After Mason finished off his wings and Simon his burger, their conversation shifted to work.

"Good job on that last project, by the way."

Mason nodded. "Thanks, man. I've got another story idea to pitch to you, something I've been looking into for a while. Remember Anthony Lackey, the congresswoman's son's drunk driving incident?"

"Yeah. He injured the other driver in the crash. Thank God the woman survived."

"Right. Rumor has it that the congresswoman paid off the local news stations and reporters to keep from running the story—no bad press since she's up for re-election."

"I'm not surprised."

"And this cover-up is just one of many. That's the next story you'll be getting from me. I've already started my research. Right now, Anthony is in the hospital for a medical procedure. Not sure if the procedure has anything to do with the injuries he sustained from his recent accident, but he's in police custody in the hospital. His DNA matches the DNA in the blood from the murder scene of Flex Technology's COO. He has an alibi, but he hasn't been cleared yet. My bet is the congresswoman has found a way to fix that situation as well."

Simon patted his shoulder. "Looks like you're back."

Now more than ever, he needed work to occupy his time and energy. A new story to investigate. Some wrongdoing to expose that authorities tried to cover up. Sometimes he got his ideas from watching the nightly news where the news anchor would report a story and move on, not diving deeper to give the citizens the truth they deserved. This story idea, he'd come across months ago because he overheard someone mentioning Congresswoman Lackey at one of his father's political fundraisers. Had his father still been alive, he may not have given the gossip a second thought.

Mason took a large gulp of his soda. "I'm doing the best I can, and work is the only thing to keep my mind focused on the fact that I've lost him." Even saying the words didn't sound right coming from his lips. And while his job kept him company during the day, his biggest problem was when he closed his eyes at night. His nightmares of what-ifs plagued him.

What if he had stayed with his father that night?

What if he'd insisted his father leave with him?

What if the ambulance had gotten to his father a minute sooner?

What if the Fire Investigator's report was wrong and someone was at fault?

And every night, the nightmares jolted him out of his disturbed sleep. Nothing would bring his father back to life.

"I understand. You know I'm here if you need me, and if you need more time off work, just say the word."

"Thanks, man."

"You know you're the best investigative journalist I have, don't you?"

Mason turned to look at Simon and quirked an eyebrow. "What's the favor?"

Simon chuckled. When he recovered, he sipped his beer before he responded, "I've hired a promising journalist with limited experience, at least in this arena. Her journalism experience dates back to college where she worked on her college newspaper staff, but after she graduated, she went on to work with her family's business in public relations."

Mason nodded and turned his attention back to the large flat-screen TV. "I see. Why'd you hire her if her experience is so limited?"

"Like I said, she's promising, works hard, and I have faith in her."

"And?"

"And, with the right mentor, she has the potential to be just as good as you."

"I thought you invited me out to watch the game. You brought me here to tell me I'll be babysitting." Every day he prayed for strength to remain focused. And while he loved his work, he couldn't see himself being in the best position to mentor anyone else right now.

Simon chuckled again. "You have to change your perspective. You're looking at it all wrong. The way I see it, there is no one else on my staff better fit for mentoring her."

"But I work alone." Well, there was that one assignment when he left to work in Washington for a while, but he didn't get a chance to see it to completion. However, that information was beside the fact. Simon knew his preferences.

Simon slapped Mason's back. "Not for the next few months you don't."

∞

The following morning, Mason sat in Simon's office in one of the visitor's chairs across from his cherry wood L-shaped desk,

18

which took up the majority of the space in his office. Though they mostly worked in an electronic environment, steel file cabinets lined one of Simon's walls. A sixteen-paned window accounted for the wall space behind Simon's desk. His office always smelled of old wood and coffee beans.

Simon leaned back in his seat and linked his fingers over his belly. "I've been thinking a lot about the story you're working on about Congresswoman Lackey. You know you have total freedom in your research and how you work your assignments, but I think having our new employee along for the ride will be beneficial to you both. She can help with the research and get first-hand experience on how the master does his job."

Mason shook his head. "I'm sitting in your office so that means I'll mentor her, so no need to stroke my ego."

"Since we're at work, I won't say how big your head is already. You don't need me to stroke your ego."

They shared a laugh.

"But I need to shoot straight. You remember the kind of illegal activity you uncovered when you left that assignment in Washington?"

Mason nodded. "What are you getting at?"

Simon leaned forward and braced his weight on the table. "This investigation of yours could get ugly and make the wrong people mad. You need to watch your back on this one, and with Ms. Langston by your side, hopefully, you'll be able to keep a level head."

Mason was already beginning to regret accepting the mentorship responsibility.

Simon lifted the phone receiver. "Please send in Ms. Langston."

A few minutes later, a soft tap sounded on Simon's doorframe. "Here's Ms. Langston," Ms. Carey, Simon's administrative assistant, announced. The white-haired woman turned away without another word.

Simon waved her inside. "Layla, please come on in."

She strolled into Simon's office and reached across the desk to shake his hand. "It's nice to see you again, Mr. Taylor."

"Call me Simon. And this," Simon gestured toward Mason, "is Mason Sterling. He'll be your mentor. I'll leave it up to Mason to do what he does. He can help get you started."

She turned to Mason with an outstretched hand and a smile as wide as Simon's laptop screen.

"I'm Layla Langston."

Mason turned his attention to eager, expectant eyes. Soft, welcoming eyes. Eyes that he found hard to look away from. He swallowed his lack of enthusiasm, stood, accepted her hand, and squeezed, probably a little too hard. In his defense, the connection he felt upon contact caught him off guard, and instead of letting go, he tightened his grip. "Mason Sterling."

"Nice to meet you." Layla smiled and loosened her grip, an unspoken way to say, *Let me go.*

"And it's nice to meet you, too. Come follow me so we can get you set up."

He'd make an exception to his working alone rule this one time as long as Layla Langston didn't get in his way. Although Simon needed a story and Layla needed to learn the ropes, Mason needed space to navigate his new life.

CHAPTER THREE

The shift from vice president of public relations at Langston Brands to a journalist at *The Houston Exposure* was not supposed to thrust Layla into the proximity of working alongside Mason Sterling. And though he was cordial, his full, tightened lips and squinted eyes made it clear he wasn't too happy about being paired with her. Even trying to hide his lack of enthusiasm, his attractive eyes weren't lost on her. The man was the epitome of tall, dark, and handsome. When he stood, his presence commanded attention, towering over her by at least ten to twelve inches. Strong shoulders and neck. The kind of neck she referred to as a football neck because she'd only noted such muscular features on football players. And his milk chocolate skin, not obstructed by facial hair, appeared smooth.

But his appearance didn't matter. And neither did that tingle that danced up her arm when they shook hands back in Simon's office. She'd be in his presence just long enough for him to train and mentor her, then she'd move on to cover her own stories, and Mason Sterling wouldn't have to worry about her being in his way ever again.

Layla trailed him down an aisle with cubicles to her left and right. Mason introduced her to journalists who were in the office. And that was only a handful of people. The environment was quiet, much like that of Langston Brands's corporate office, with the tapping of fingertips along the keyboards loud to her ears. And although *The Houston Exposure*'s operations were purely digital, the space smelled of hot copy paper, or was she imagining it?

"Nice to meet you, Layla. I'm Maya." The black woman appeared to be around forty years old, same age as Layla. Maya smiled and shook her hand. As a minority in the office space, it was nice to meet someone who seemed kind and who looked like her. But Maya's presence was also a reminder that she left familiarity behind at Langston Brands in search of her own path.

"Thanks, Maya. Nice to meet you as well. How long have you been with *The Houston Exposure*?"

"Seems like forever, but it's only been about ten years. Mason's been around for ages, so I'm sure he has you covered. However, I'm around if you have any questions or need help with anything."

"I'll remember that. Thanks."

Maya plopped down into her chair. "I'm going to get back to work. I need to get this story to Simon before I go on vacation."

"We won't hold you up. Thanks, Maya," Mason said.

He led Layla past two more sets of cubicles before he stopped at his desk. "This is my cubicle. You'll sit there." He pointed to the other side of the aisle.

Layla placed her purse on the desk and clasped her hands. "Okay. What do we do first?"

Mason gestured toward her chair. "Please have a seat."

He sat and linked his fingers together. Layla knew his type. Worked alone and probably felt like he didn't need anyone's help. She held her breath and prepared to hear his this-is-how-things-are-gonna-go speech.

"Tell me about you and your background, Layla Langston." She detected a bit of a Nigerian accent. His tone was soft and inquisitive, almost as if he was interviewing her, but also more welcoming than she expected.

Oh.

Layla sat and met his gaze. Tension she didn't realize she had eased from her body. "I have a master's degree in communications. For nearly twenty years, I've worked for my family's luxury handbag business, Langston Brands. When I left, my position was vice president of public relations."

Mason nodded.

She assumed he was thinking of all the ways he'd have to train her, so she defended herself, not that she needed to because she already had the job. But there was something about the inquisitive look on his face that made her want to explain more. "Don't worry. I'm a quick learner, and I'm naturally inquisitive. You won't have to spend too much time training me, and I'll be out of your hair in no time."

"I never said training you was a problem."

"No, you didn't, but I can read body language well, and yours is saying you'd much rather be working on your assignment than sitting here teaching me how to ride without training wheels."

Mason threw his head back and laughed. Weird, but Layla enjoyed the man before her whose scowl had been replaced with more relaxed features and the showing of his teeth. And it didn't help that his laugh was contagious. Layla chuckled, too.

He tapped his chest. "I'm sorry if I'm giving bad vibes. Personally, I'm dealing with a lot, and Simon's request for me to mentor you came as a surprise."

"Why is that?"

"I'm used to working alone. I do my best work that way, part of the reason I enjoy the gig so much."

"Well, the way I see it, if you're a good on-the-job instructor and we work well together, you can help me learn what I need to get going on my own and I can help you with your current assignment, then before you know it, you'll be back to doing your best solo work."

He smiled with his eyes. Something transpired in his head that he chose not to share. Layla could deal with him not sharing his thoughts, which would likely lead to more banter. As much as he preferred solo projects, Layla had a feeling he'd be her work bestie by the time he finished training her.

∞

Mason had only known Layla fifteen minutes, and she was already working her way through his emotional defenses, peeling back the protective layers. Beautiful and lighthearted. Though it

25

seemed they wouldn't have any problems getting along, he could only hope she wouldn't be a distraction.

"Do you really think Simon would have paired you with me if I wasn't the best?"

She shrugged, and a smile spread across her lips—the kind of smile that shouted whatever she was about to say would probably be challenging, smart-mouthed, and funny. "I don't know. Maybe you were the only one available. Maya did say that she's heading out on vacation. Everyone else I met a while ago seemed to be busy, too."

Mason laughed much more in the past few minutes than he had in the past few months. "Let's just clear this up right now then: You've got the best."

If he didn't know any better, he'd think she'd been intentionally baiting him. Mason pushed away from her cubicle, his chair rolling back toward his own desk. He grabbed his laptop and slid back over to her.

"Here, let me show you what we'll be working on."

Mason flipped the lid and clicked around the screen until he opened the file labeled *Congresswoman Lackey*. He gave her a few minutes to read the case highlights and his notes before he began with his spiel. Layla nodded and turned toward him with wide eyes.

"Wow. This is going to be interesting. The congresswoman covering up a string of crimes, including her son's possible involvement in a murder. Who would've thought?" Layla leaned in close. "How'd you come across this story?"

"I just happened to be in the right place at the right time to hear some gossip and decided to look into it. Other stories I've pitched often come from watching the nightly news or reading the paper. It's important for you to keep your eyes open. A story idea can come from anywhere."

"Gotcha. So, you have the story idea and your notes here. How do you typically start your research?"

"Public sources. Everything you see in this file has come from news stories about her in the last five years. The information about her son was leaked from someone in her camp because she's done a good job of keeping the news outlets from running the story."

She had an expectant look in her eyes. "What's next?"

"This is where I can use your help. We need to figure out where Anthony Lackey was on the night of the murder, follow up on his alibi, and gather every piece of information that exists about him." He counted off on his fingers. "Since this is the congresswoman's most recent cover-up—at least that we know about—we should start with her son. She couldn't hide this from the public alone. She needs help from inside the police department, and I'm of the opinion that whatever she's up to runs deeper than her re-election."

"You really are good at your job. Sounds like you're off to a good start."

"Thanks. This is how we learn the story behind the story, by digging deeper to find out what his family and the police don't want us to know."

Layla clasped her hands in her lap. She still held that gleam in her eyes. "I'm excited. Put me to work."

Mason raised a palm. "I should caution you that sniffing around politicians can possibly put us in harm's way. As with anything, we don't know what we're walking into or who we might upset when we start digging deeper and asking more questions. If this makes you uncomfortable, I can talk with Simon about having someone else mentor you."

Layla held his gaze and squinted. "Trying to get rid of me? I thought we established an understanding."

"Not trying to get rid of you anymore." He paused to gauge her reaction. Just like he thought, she tossed her head back and laughed. Mason joined in. "Seriously, I just want you to know what you're getting into."

"I understand. Call me weird, but it's a little exciting if you ask me. I know exactly what I'm getting into."

There was no way Layla could understand or be prepared for the journey ahead or how far he was willing to go to get the information he needed to expose the congresswoman and her family. This was no ordinary assignment, which meant he'd take extraordinary steps at every opportunity. He'd tried to warn her, hadn't he? Whatever the case, he'd see what she was made of. Mason could only hope that she'd be a help and not a hindrance in this investigation.

"Okay then. Let's get to work."

CHAPTER FOUR

Layla had spent the last three-and-a-half days performing research for Mason's case involving Congresswoman Lackey and her son. She'd arrived at work thirty minutes early this morning to review her notes for their meeting. Reporting to someone other than her sister, Crystal, would take some getting used to. And although her big sister was her boss at Langston Brands, working with Crystal and Ava was more like co-piloting. Although Crystal was in charge, she often sought the advice of both Ava and Layla before making a final decision. But this morning Layla felt like she had to prepare the perfect assignment to hand in to her teacher to earn an A.

She convinced herself that Mason's opinion wasn't too important, but in the same heartbeat, she wanted to make a positive impression. Surely Mason would be reporting back to Simon with details of her progress.

Not only did she prepare for this morning's meeting, but out of curiosity, she'd done her research on Mason as well. When they met, the last name Sterling sounded familiar, but she couldn't recall why until she learned that his father was Walter Sterling—the man running against Congresswoman Lackey. He'd been killed after a building explosion at his last political fundraiser.

Could Mason's story about Congresswoman Lackey somehow be fueled by what happened to his father? It didn't seem appropriate to ask him such a question, so she'd keep the thought to herself.

She checked the time. Mason should arrive in fifteen minutes, so she continued skimming her notes. Her research of the congresswoman's son, Anthony Lackey, revealed he'd had a couple of DUIs that have been kept under wraps. She'd identified and located known associates in case Mason wanted to interview them. Anthony also worked on his mother's campaign and was often seen as part of her security detail, which meant that she didn't go too far without him by her side.

Mason's heavy footsteps grew closer. Without looking around her cubicle, she knew it was him. For one, their cubicles were in the back of the area. No spaces were behind them. And two, she could sense his presence. Why he had that effect on her, she couldn't be sure.

"Good morning."

Layla looked up. Mason strolled in wearing a crisp white buttoned shirt, black slacks. No tie. He dressed in a similar fashion every day. His smiling eyes silently challenged her to see whether her research skills were up to par. Did he somehow doubt her abilities?

"Good morning, Mason. I'm ready for our meeting when you are."

She crossed her legs and stretched back in her seat before taking a sip of her morning coffee. One thing he'd never be able to say about her was that she was unprepared or incapable.

He gave her a once-over and nodded. "I'm sure you are. I doubt you'd show up early dressed like you're ready to take over the world if you weren't." Mason winked and turned his back to her. Layla watched him remove his backpack, unpack, and set up his laptop. She shouldn't take the winking gesture for more than it was, but her mind couldn't help but wonder what he meant by it. Did he wink often? Was that trademark Mason behavior? It didn't matter.

"I appreciate the vote of confidence."

Mason slid his chair across the carpet into her cubicle space as he'd done every day when he wanted to discuss the project, show her an article on his computer, or demonstrate some sort of office procedure. While she enjoyed the hands-on training, his closeness affected her in a way she hadn't anticipated. His scent was a mix of cedar, soap, and masculinity. His accent mesmerized her—a deep smooth sound. She could listen to him read the dictionary. And she was attracted to his passion for his work. On top of that, the man was handsome and confident. Mason didn't strike her as the kind of person who needed to prove he was at the top of his game.

His lips spread into that stomach-churning smile again. "I have no problem giving props when props are due. I trust Simon more than anyone, and he speaks highly of you. If he says you're the one, then you're the one. Let's go through what came of your research." He folded his arms across his chest and nodded, as if saying it was okay for her to continue.

31

Tearing her wondering thoughts away from the hypnotization of his smooth voice, Layla turned her attention to her laptop. "Yes, so I started with your notes about Congresswoman Lackey and spent some time looking into her son, Anthony." Layla gave him a thorough update on what she'd learned. She paused and thought for a moment. "Okay, this just came to me. What if her son is like her henchman or something—doing her dirty work for her? I'd like to believe that something like that wouldn't be happening in real life, but it's possible they're working together to hide something."

She stared into his eyes and waited for his reaction.

Mason hiked an eyebrow.

"I like you, Layla Langston. Great minds think alike. That's exactly what we're going to find out."

∞

Every second he listened to Layla speak, Mason became more impressed. As much as he didn't like the idea of being a mentor right now, he had to admit that having another person around to bounce ideas off energized him. And not just any person, but Layla. Something about her captivated him. A small part of him didn't want to like her simply because he'd been blindsided by the fact that he'd be working with her. He'd dubbed her the monkey wrench in his plans. However, Layla had already proven herself useful. Perhaps she'd been the missing link—what he needed all along—in his investigation. He'd been looking into Congresswoman Lackey on his own, but now with more brainpower, Mason might finally be able to satisfy his own curiosity and present the public with the answers they deserved.

"I have an idea. Why don't we talk to the detective who worked the scene of Anthony's car crash? I know the other driver survived, but it's possible the detective was involved in ensuring the situation wasn't made public."

He pushed his chair back toward his cubicle to retrieve his laptop. After he reclaimed his space in Layla's area, he highlighted the first item on his list and opened his laptop toward her. "I couldn't agree more. Detective Juanita Mansfield is who I want to talk to first."

Layla lifted a palm in the air for him to high-five her. "C'mon, you know you want to. We're so in sync."

Mason shook his head, but indulged her anyway. When their palms connected, he felt the synchronization between them. Every part of him did. His heart. His mind. His entire being echoed from the brevity of the moment.

The excitement and light in her eyes set his heart on fire. His chest burned from his heart's gallop. Mason rubbed the area, almost certain that Layla could see the pulsing of his chest.

She slid her laptop closer and opened a Word document. "Let's draft up some interview questions. We may only get one shot to talk to her, and we want to make sure we don't miss anything."

"Woman, you're on fire this morning. I've already started with my questions. I'll forward you what I have, and we can work from my copy."

Mason e-mailed the file to Layla. Once she received and opened the document, she took a couple of minutes to read through the interview questions he'd already come up with. Reading his thoughts lit a spark in her because she became a bubbling fountain of ideas. Talking with her was easy, and after a couple hours had passed, Mason realized he could talk to her all day. Several times, they veered off topic and talked about things unrelated to the case—crime shows they liked to watch. Favorite foods—hers being salmon and his being most seafood. And her sisters. In fact, she mentioned her sisters about three times. Mason assumed they were close. He'd be surprised if they weren't, considering they worked together and spent even more time as a family outside of business.

"Think we have enough? I don't mind continuing to work, but I'd prefer to do so over lunch."

Mason flipped his wrist to check the time. "It is about that time. Since you're also a seafood lover, I take it you want to go to a restaurant that serves a really good grilled salmon."

Layla's lips curved into a smile. "That sounds good, but I'm flexible."

Mason stood and rolled his chair back to his own cubicle. "I know just the spot. If you don't mind, I'll drive." He hesitated after the offer slipped from his lips. They'd been involved in such great conversation that suggesting she ride with him seemed natural. Besides, they were coworkers, so going out to lunch together wasn't odd—in the twelve years he'd worked at *The Houston Exposure,* he hadn't invited any woman into his vehicle for lunch. But he could justify that, too, because he always worked alone.

34

While his mind wandered whether the suggestion for her to ride with him was awkward, it didn't seem as if Layla gave it a second thought. "That works. I'm going to run to the ladies' room and meet you at the elevator bank."

Before she left, Layla packed her laptop into her portfolio bag and handed it to him for safekeeping. He stuffed his own laptop into his backpack and walked to the elevator bank to wait for her. And for every minute she was away, he thought of her—thought of how much of a great team they made. Had Simon known they'd be good together? Mason would never admit to Simon that Layla had already grown on him. The opportunity to work with her might be equally as exciting as getting the answers he sought. Exposing the Congresswoman could be huge for his career, but he'd have to be careful not to allow the beautiful distraction and connection he shared with Layla Langston to interfere with that.

CHAPTER FIVE

Layla shouldn't be nervous about riding shotgun in Mason's truck, especially after how well they'd worked together that morning, but she was.

Nervous that the drive might be awkward at times when bouts of silence filled the cabin.

Nervous about what he thought of her—why his opinion mattered, she couldn't be certain.

And nervous because being with him felt like spending time with an old friend. Weird how connected she and Mason seemed to be.

Because being in his presence felt a lot like hanging out with someone she'd known for years. The drive to Goode Company Seafood had been a breeze. Turns out, her brief stint of worry had been in vain. When Mason turned into the restaurant's parking lot, it felt like they'd just climbed into his truck instead of riding for the last twenty-three minutes.

Would time with him always feel this way? Good and easy. Familiar. Or was he on his best behavior because of their new working relationship? If he was just being cordial, her heart would likely become putty in his hands if things were any better between them when he became his true self.

Mason parked and hurried around to the passenger's side to open the door for her before she could completely unbuckle her seatbelt and grab her handbag. Layla's eyes met his. She didn't get the feeling there were any romantic undertones in his behavior—he only did what came natural to him. This would be a working lunch, so why did she even consider for a moment that this was anything more? The thought wouldn't have crossed her mind if she were at Langston Brands where she sometimes had working lunches with male colleagues.

But none of them looked like Mason or made her heart skip a beat here and there either.

"Let's get you that fish," he said when she climbed out of the truck.

She appreciated that he listened to her go on about her disappointment in last night's fish dinner from another popular Houston restaurant. How their conversation went from interview questions for Detective Juanita Mansfield to fish dinners, she couldn't be sure. The one certainty in all of this was that Mason was easy to talk to. Or maybe she'd just been accustomed to talking to her sisters about any and everything that she now used Mason as a replacement. She was still adjusting to life outside of Langston Brands, but he didn't seem to mind.

"I already know what I'm going to order."

Mason closed the door. "Same. Mesquite grilled salmon for me."

Layla chuckled. "Get out of my head. That's exactly what I plan to order in hopes that this meal will make up for the not-so-good one last night."

Mason's lips curled into a knowing smile—a smile she could get used to and preferred compared to the half-scowl he wore when they met in Simon's office earlier that week. "C'mon. I've got you."

Layla scrunched her eyebrows and pouted. Thank goodness she walked in front of Mason to hide her facial expression, which she couldn't help. It was the face she made when she questioned if the person she was in conversation with was aware of what they were saying. She shrugged it off though. Simon wasn't paying her to analyze Mason.

After they were seated and placed their orders, Layla removed her laptop from her bag to set up on the table next to her place setting. Because they planned a working lunch, Layla requested a booth for the added table space. Besides, a small intimate table for two didn't seem to be the best idea considering her wandering thoughts about whether he meant more by his words and gestures.

When their waitress brought their waters and disappeared, Layla read through the questions they'd collaborated on that morning. "I think we're off to a solid start with our line of questioning. I honestly can't think of anything else to ask."

Mason nodded. "How are your interview skills?"

"Back in college, I conducted interviews for my college newspaper, but I'm a bit rusty. I haven't flexed those skills in recent years."

"I see. That's a good start. Keep in mind that it's important to read people and know when they're lying to you or hiding information."

"I can pretty much sense when someone isn't being truthful—not giving eye contact, primarily shifting their eyes to the left. Body language. Changes in their tone of voice."

"Detective Langston is what I should be calling you then."

Laughter bubbled from Layla's throat. "Nah, but I appreciate the compliment." Not to mention she had experience with the shifty behaviors of folks coming for her family over the past few years, but she refused to get into that line of conversation.

"There's not much else we need to add right now, but more ideas always come to mind during the interview, so it's important to listen to what she says and doesn't say. And don't allow her to rush you. Take your time. We have plenty unless she kicks us out."

Layla's breath caught. She leaned forward and whispered, unsure of why she felt the need to lower her voice. "Do you really think she'd put us out?"

Mason sipped his water and shrugged. "I don't know. Not everyone wants to talk to journalists. In fact, most folks don't. And in this case, we'll likely receive some pushback if what we suspect is true."

"You mean if she's been somehow helping the congresswoman cover up her son's misdeeds?"

"Right. And maybe she even helped the congresswoman conceal her own."

"All will be well. We make a great team so we'll figure this out together."

∞

Mason didn't share the same confidence as Layla—that of a newbie. In a perfect world, all would be well. They'd conduct interviews, gather all the information needed, write the story, expose the congresswoman's string of wrongdoings, and move on. But this project wouldn't be that easy. He'd bet his retirement on it. However, this would be the perfect experience for Layla.

The waitress returned with their entrees. Mason blessed their food, and they ate in comfortable silence for the first few minutes.

"Does your salmon make up for last night?"

Layla pointed to her half-empty plate. "If this isn't evidence enough, I don't know what is."

Mason chuckled. "Yeah, this is good." He took another bite. After he'd chewed and swallowed, he asked, "So do you have any questions for me? Any concerns about the interview? We're driving out to Galveston tomorrow to pay Detective Mansfield a visit."

"No questions yet. I probably won't have any until after it's all over." She paused a beat. "Honestly, I'm weirdly excited about this interview, probably because of the freshness of the job and this new phase in my career."

Mason had performed an online search of Layla and her family's business last night. From what he could glean, Langston Brands was thriving, and her relationship with her family seemed stable based on their earlier conversations, so this change in career for her had him curious. Based on his conversation with Simon

40

about her work history, he assumed she was around forty years old. Was she going through some type of midlife crisis?

Mason massaged his chin with his thumb and forefinger. They would be working together for a while, so it was only fair that he know more about her. "I hope you find your career in journalism as rewarding as I do, but I am curious, why the switch now?"

Layla glanced around the restaurant before she met his gaze and shrugged. "I want something for myself."

Mason sipped his water, leaned back in his seat, and folded his arms across his chest. He nodded in her direction. "Explain."

Her eyes gleamed a little, as if she'd been waiting for him to ask the question. Layla flipped her wrist to check the time on her watch. "How much time do you have?"

He waved his hand. "For you, as much time as you need."

Layla huffed, and a half-chuckle escaped her lips. Her lips spread into a wide smile. And that is when the thought crossed his mind—he could talk and listen to her all day. But they were at work, and she was his protégé of sorts, so Mason withdrew from the line of thought.

"Before I went to college, it was understood that my studies would lead me back to my family's company. For me, my sisters Crystal and Ava, we were to go to college, earn degrees, come home to learn, and one day run the family's business. And Langston Brands has grown so much that we're hardly a small business anymore. My sisters both have a life outside of Langston Brands, both being newly married and one with a child coming soon. I believe I owe it to myself to do something I've always wanted to do.

41

And I've always wanted a career in journalism, so this is the best time for me to try something different. I can always go back if my career here doesn't work out."

"How did your family feel about you leaving?"

"They weren't thrilled, but they all support my decision."

"I'm impressed. Starting over takes courage." Mason raised his water glass. "Cheers to you for trying something new."

Layla raised her water glass and clinked it against his. "Thank you."

"I might not be as fun to work with at times, but whatever I can do to make this transition easier for you, just say the word."

"I appreciate that, Mason, but I have a feeling you're more fun to work with than you realize."

"We'll see if you're singing the same tune in a couple of weeks."

Layla leaned forward in her seat. The twinkle in her eye sparkled. "Oh, I will because you want to make a good impression. You don't strike me as the kind of man who would be unprofessional and allow a bad attitude to get in the way of your work. You, Mason Sterling, believe you're the best, and you wouldn't do anything to undermine that fact."

Mason rested his back against the plush seating in the booth. "*Hmmmp.* You think you know me, huh?"

"Not fully, but I'm not wrong."

From the satisfied smirk poised on the corner of her upturned lip, he'd go as far as to say that she was hoping to get a rise out of him. She'd held his gaze as if in a showdown. When she saw he wouldn't take the bait, she asked, "So what's the game plan for tomorrow?"

"We have about an hour's drive, so I'll pick you up at eight, then we can stop for breakfast before hitting the road."

"I can be ready at eight. What if she doesn't talk to us?"

"I have a feeling we won't have to worry about that. We'll get some information from her, though it may not be as much as we'd like."

"And you're comfortable showing up at her house unannounced? How do you know she'll be home?"

"First, Simon has word that she's on leave this week. Second, Detective Mansfield knows who I am. We met early on in my career, and she's been a valuable contact. I wouldn't be surprised if she's expecting me, given Anthony Lackey's latest infraction. She knows me well enough to understand that I'm always on top of a good story." When Layla didn't seem moved by his explanation, he added, "We spoke a month ago concerning my suspicions about the congresswoman, but she didn't give me anything I didn't already know. Let's hope she'll have more answers for me this time."

"I'm not keen with popping up on someone's doorstep without calling first, but I understand your method, and I trust you know what you're doing. Besides, this is what I signed up for, so I'm all in."

"Good because that's the type of attitude that'll take you far in your journalism career."

"Plus, the fact that I have the right teacher…"

Though he didn't need it, she'd just stroked his ego. Mason smiled. "I couldn't agree more."

He paid for their lunches and drove Layla back to the office, where they discussed potential local community stories for her to cover as part of her first solo piece. After their meeting, he left her to continue her own research on the congresswoman project. She promised to get them a sit-down with District Attorney Marcel Singleton, who was also her brother-in-law, to discuss where his office stood on the issue of both Anthony Lackey and Congresswoman Lackey's crimes.

Layla impressed him because she didn't need him as much. Part of him appreciated her independence but also didn't like she wasn't as dependent on him. And he knew that wanting her to need him was crazy, but his thoughts ran rampant on the matter. Soon enough, she'd just be another coworker he'd see in the office every now and then, and he already didn't like that idea.

Mason pushed those thoughts aside to focus on his face-to-face with Detective Mansfield. His relationship with her wasn't as good as he'd led Layla to believe. In fact, the woman probably hated to see him coming. She'd always referred to him as a troublemaker who would one day make her lose her job, yet she continued to feed him information when he needed her. The last time they talked, she brushed off his speculation about the Lackeys, but he knew she was hiding something.

He hoped tomorrow would weave a different story and she'd confirm his hunch.

CHAPTER SIX

*B*ack inside of the pine box, Layla couldn't move or speak—almost one with the piece of wood beneath her, though she couldn't verify anything because she couldn't move her head. All she could see was the covering above her. Her heart slammed a quick, rhythmic thud in her chest and ears. How'd she end up back in here? This time, she had no wiggle room. She couldn't fan her fingers or move her toes. The only part of her body she could move was her eyes. Last time she'd been trapped inside of the box, the darkness was thick and heavy, but today she saw a sliver of light.

Light meant hope.

In the distance, she heard a voice. Layla strained to understand what was being said. Hopefully, someone would notice her if they were close enough for her to hear them. She waited, not that she had much of a choice, and prayed.

Lord, please send help. Don't let me die in here.

That's when she associated the voice with....Juanita Mansfield. But how could this be? She hadn't met her yet, had she?

"Minding other folks' business is what got her into this mess. She shouldn't be here. You shouldn't be here, either. Leave while you still have the chance. Leave the past in the past."

When had she stuck her nose in someone else's business? She didn't even know these people.

This can't be real.

This can't be real.

This cannot be real.

Footsteps drew closer. She'd had the morbid thought that she'd been buried until hearing the sound of hardwood beneath the footsteps. Her breathing grew ragged and heavy. Who was it and what were they planning to do with her? And who was Juanita Mansfield talking to?

The top of the box slid open. More light filtered through. The face of her rescuer—or captor, she couldn't be sure who it was and whose side they were on—was blurry.

Before she could get a clear picture of the face, she woke up, toppling to the floor from the bed, like she'd been thrown from one reality into another. The romance novel she'd been reading before drifting to sleep fell into her lap.

Dread crept into her heart. Changing careers was supposed to bring her peace, not put her smack dab in the middle of someone's drama. To think rationally, she'd had these dreams long before she changed careers or met Mason Sterling or heard anything about Detective Mansfield. Maybe the dream was just a manifestation of her unaddressed anxiety about meeting the woman today.

A chill cut through her entire being. Layla shook her head and shoulders before she stood. *I am not going to allow any crazy dreams to interfere with my peace.* After all, peace, purpose, and direction were what she was after. But she couldn't deceive herself. That dream now had her curious about the woman. What was Layla walking into today? And what had Detective Mansfield been up to?

Her phone alarm sounded, cutting through her wandering thoughts about Detective Mansfield and reminded her to get ready for her road trip down to Galveston with Mason. And what about Mason? Should she tell him about her vivid visions? Sometimes they were off, but most of the time, they were spot-on. However, she didn't quite know what this set of dreams meant or how she would explain such dreams—or nightmares—to him. Would he think she'd lost her mind?

While she dressed in what she liked to call her dressy jeans, black ruffle blouse, and ballet flats, Layla tried to push the nightmare images aside. She'd grabbed her blazer and brewed herself a cup of coffee with hopes that the hot liquid would melt the thoughts away so she wouldn't wear a spooky expression when Mason showed up on her doorstep in the next ten minutes.

When the coffee maker completed the brewing process, she didn't wait to sip as she normally would. She added French Vanilla creamer, a half teaspoon of sugar, and two ice cubes. With trembling fingers, she lifted the mug to her lips. The simple act of drinking her morning brew now served as a distraction. At some point, she'd have to tell him about what her dreams revealed if this investigation got out of control. Was it crazy to think her dreams could be a clue?

And if that were the case, hopefully what she saw when her eyes were closed wasn't literal. Being bound and trapped in a box wasn't her idea of starting a new career to have something for herself.

Two minutes, and Layla finished off her coffee, something she was certain she'd never done in such a short amount of time. In her powder room, she double checked her reflection, applied her favorite shade of red lipstick, and headed into the living room at the sound of the doorbell.

Layla opened the front door, and her mouth went dry, possibly from the coffee, but most likely because of Mason standing before her with his come-hither smile. Of course, he didn't intend to make her heart play double Dutch, but that fact didn't matter. Her surroundings faded into the background at the sight of him in blue jeans and a muscle-hugging short-sleeved polo shirt—relatively ordinary clothes. A look she'd seen on plenty of men. But the way Mason wore it was different.

However, she wouldn't be overcome or distracted by his good looks. She had work to do and a point to prove to herself, Mason, her family, and Simon. She could do this job—live outside of her family's image, create a life for herself—and do it well.

"Hey. Good morning. You're right on time."

His eyes scanned her, and an appreciative smile formed on his lips, drawing a similar reaction from her. Mason stood at her doorstep with his hands stuffed in his pockets. "Good morning. Are you ready?"

"Yep." She slung her crossbody purse over her shoulder, grabbed her portfolio bag, and stepped outside. The lock automatically engaged when she closed the door.

"After you."

Mason led her to his truck and opened the door for her. Once inside himself, he turned to Layla before starting the ignition. "You okay? Something seems different about you today."

Perhaps she'd done a poor job of hiding the apprehension that rose within her from last night's nightmare. But she couldn't say anything to him about it, especially not when she couldn't make sense of it herself just yet. She swallowed her discomfort.

"I'm fine. Ready to see what the day will bring. What are you thinking for breakfast, something quick or dine-in?"

She hoped switching the subject would encourage him not to push the matter. But then she regretted bringing about the dine-in idea. Sitting down to eat would only give him more time to analyze her and ask questions. And like he once told her, he always got his answers, but she was good at hiding her emotions, right?

"Toasted Yolk sounds good. I love their pancakes. Does that work for you?"

"They serve an Alaskan Arnold that I like."

"Perfect." He typed the restaurant into his phone's GPS. "There's one about fifteen minutes away along our route."

Mason shifted his truck into gear and backed out of her driveway. Like yesterday's car ride, this morning's trip was also easy. He'd casted a few concerned glances her way, which meant he didn't buy her *I'm fine* response. If he only knew that he was making matters worse by his concern, maybe he'd stop looking at her with wrinkled eyebrows and caring eyes. That look was what kept her mind trapped in that wooden box. And she was trying to forget.

She needed to forget.

∞

Something was different about Layla this morning. Though her mouth said she was fine, her eyes hadn't received the message. He couldn't be sure if what he saw in her eyes was fear or apprehension or something else, neither of which matched her demeanor from yesterday. Yesterday's Layla seemed excited and ready to tackle something new. Today's Layla looked like she wanted to turn around and run. But why?

Mason didn't know her well enough to push the issue. It was not his intent to make her uncomfortable, only he needed her at her best in this investigation. Layla knew as much, so he had to trust she wouldn't allow anything to hinder her work.

Once inside the restaurant with their orders placed, Mason had to ask one more time. Though Layla tried to mask her feelings, he didn't buy the front she put on.

"Layla, are you sure you're up for this trip? I have no problem going alone while you stick around here to chat with the DA."

"Thanks for offering a way out, but I told you I'm all in. I'm good. Just had a bad dream last night is all. Nothing to worry about."

She lifted her coffee mug to her lips and peered at him over the rim, no doubt trying to hide her facial expression.

"We're spending all day together. Plenty of time for you to share the bad dream if it'll make you feel better. Isn't there a saying that if you talk about your dreams—or nightmares—they won't happen?"

Something flashed in her eyes, like she considered whether she should reveal her sleeping thoughts, but then she shook her head. "No, nothing to share really. It actually didn't even make sense. I'm fine. Trust me."

Trust her.

He wanted to trust her. In fact, he needed to trust her for them to work well together. He held her gaze for a while after but had to withdraw and turn his attention away. The more he looked into her eyes, the more questions he had and the more he wanted to know, but on a personal level—a level that didn't matter for them to do their jobs well.

"Okay, but can we agree that you'll tell me if something is bothering you, especially if it's about our work?"

"That's a reasonable request. I won't allow anything to get in the way of us working well together."

A short, lively waitress with shoulder-length braids interrupted their conversation. "I'm back to make your morning with a delicious Alaskan Arnold, Hollandaise sauce on the side, and a fresh stack of pancakes." She placed the plates on the table in front of them. "Careful. Hot plates." With a big smile on her face, she jammed her fists into her hips and addressed Layla, but nodded toward Mason. "Is he really going to eat all of those pancakes?"

Layla took one look at a stack of three pancakes the size of his plate and laughed. "I don't know, but I'd like to see him try. He's got a long day ahead of him."

"Oh, I will. Pancakes are my favorite."

"Don't hurt yourself now," the waitress with a name tag that read Jackie tossed over her shoulder before she sauntered off to another table.

The conversation between Mason and Layla was easy for the duration of breakfast, and he appreciated Layla was becoming someone he could talk to about any topic. While she agreed they would talk about anything work related bothering her, he watched her closely for any change in her demeanor. The something-is-bothering-me look in her eyes faded. And he should be thankful she seemed to be doing better or had let go of whatever it was, but Mason couldn't shake the nagging feeling in the back of his head that whispered something was wrong.

But perhaps that feeling had nothing to do with Layla at all.

Maybe his internal discomfort settled around what would come of his interview with Detective Mansfield today. Mason saw her as an essential part of his investigation. At this juncture, in his mind, her interview was key in helping him move forward. She knew more than what she shared with him over the last month.

"Mason, where are you from? I detect a bit of a Nigerian accent."

"Are you sure? I was born and raised in Texas."

His response tickled her.

He chuckled as well. "What? I'm being serious. But my mom was Nigerian, so I suppose I picked up the accent from her."

"I can see that. It's Nigerian-Texas-American, if that's a thing. Either way, I like it."

"Thank you." He'd received numerous compliments about his accent over the years, but coming from Layla, he appreciated it a little more.

Layla finished off her breakfast and cast wide eyes at Mason. "I seriously cannot believe you ate all of that. Am I going to have to take over and drive?"

Mason chuckled. "Nope. Pancakes are my favorite. I could eat these every morning, but I know it isn't any good for me. Today's cheat day."

"And what does that mean?"

"One day a week, I choose to eat whatever I want without going overboard. Pancakes are usually on the menu for breakfast on cheat days after my morning workout."

"I may have to invite you to my Saturday morning kickboxing class one day to see what you've got."

Kickboxing wasn't his type of exercise, but he'd attend simply to see Layla in action. He'd pictured her to be more of someone who practiced yoga than someone throwing jabs and sending roundhouse kicks.

"Ready whenever you are—for kickboxing and to make this drive down to Galveston."

Layla finished her coffee and stood. "See. We're going to be best buddies by the time this is all over. I can feel it."

CHAPTER SEVEN

Mason parked his truck in one of the visitors' parking spaces outside of Detective Mansfield's oceanfront condo building.

The community's buildings were painted either yellow, blue, or green, with the detective's building being an ocean blue. The front faced the ocean, while the rear faced an open green space. From where he was parked, he could hear the waves crashing against the shore. An overwhelming sense of peace washed over him, but he couldn't be sure how long it would last. There was no telling what lay ahead of him once he knocked on her door.

He took a deep breath and turned to Layla. "Any questions before we make our presence known?"

Confidence and a sense of eagerness radiated from her. "The only questions I have are for the detective."

"Then let's do this."

Mason hopped out of his truck and rounded the bumper to open Layla's door. The slight breeze caught him off guard, especially considering when he left Houston an hour ago, it was already warm with zero signs of any kind of chill passing through. He glanced down at her flat shoes, which looked to have little comfort. "She's on the third floor. Stairs or elevator?"

Layla flexed her feet. "I came prepared. I'm good with the stairs."

Instinctively, he placed his palm at the small of her back and guided her toward the staircase, which led to Detective Mansfield's condo, according to the numbers on the building. Mason and Layla climbed three flights of stairs, turned left, and walked until they stopped in front of door 308.

His heartbeat thumped, sounding like the pace of a horse's hooves in a race. The sound was loud to his own ears. He was certain he hadn't experienced such a thing since learning of his father's death. This case was supposed to distract him from his grief, not materialize it. He came here hoping for answers about the Lackeys, but in the deep recesses of his mind, he held resentment toward Houston Police Department's detectives and the Fire Investigator who investigated the explosion that killed his father. While he couldn't prove it, Mason didn't believe they'd done a thorough job investigating the cause. The unsettling feeling in his heart told him there was more to the story.

Layla must have sensed that he needed a moment because she didn't knock on the door or ring the doorbell. She gave a nod so he could do so when ready.

Focus, Mason.

He pressed the vertical rectangle button planted on the right side of her door. He could hear the echoing chime of the doorbell outside. In Mason's mind, it felt like it had been long enough for him to run down the stairs, jump in his car and drive around the community and come back before she answered. In real time, it was more like fifteen seconds or so. Detective Juanita Mansfield opened the door and stared into his eyes. He didn't detect an ounce of surprise in her features. She stood close to Layla's height, maybe an inch taller, with a curly black afro. A few touches of gray were noticeable.

"Mason Sterling," she said. "I wondered how long it would take before I received a visit from you. Although I'm surprised by the house call." She turned her attention to Layla who thrust her palm toward the detective.

"I'm Layla Langston. We're here to ask you a few questions, if you don't mind."

Detective Mansfield gave Layla's hand a slow shake while she sized her up. "So, Lamont Langston finally let you loose." She dropped Layla's hand and stepped aside. "Well, come on in." Before she closed the door, she peered to the left and the right as if to make sure no one else was outside.

She shut the door. "Were you followed?"

Mason and Layla exchanged looks before he said, "No. Why would anyone be following us?"

"I imagine you aren't the only two who have questions with the latest reports about the congresswoman's son's DNA at the murder scene of one of Houston's top businessmen." She gestured for them to sit while she walked past them toward the kitchen. "Water or coffee?"

The aroma of fresh coffee beans filled the air, coupled with the thick smell of saltwater drifting in from the open kitchen balcony door. Her furniture matched the gray walls. In fact, nothing stood out. The house looked more like a rental or model home than one personalized to her tastes. But maybe she hadn't decorated it herself. He had no way of knowing for sure.

"I'll take water." Mason looked at Layla, who nodded for the same. "Waters for both of us."

Mason and Layla made themselves comfortable on Detective Mansfield's gray sofa and exchanged glances again. Though they didn't speak, he would bet they had the same questions. Who else had questions? How did she know Layla's father? Though that wasn't a stretch considering he was well known in the Houston area because of Langston Brands. Was Detective Mansfield expecting anyone else to show up? Who did she think would be following them? And would she share any of that information?

Dressed in a tracksuit with three stripes down the sides, Detective Mansfield returned with two bottles of water and a cup of coffee for herself. She sat in the adjacent accent chair, half-slouched like she'd been through this conversation a hundred times already and looked between the two of them. "So, you have questions for me?"

Layla swiped her finger over the screen of her electronic tablet. "Congresswoman Lackey's son, Anthony, is currently under police surveillance at the hospital. If he has an alibi the night of the murder in question, why is he under surveillance? Is he a suspect for another crime?"

Mason watched the detective's body language, which hadn't changed. She seemed relaxed—almost too relaxed for his liking.

"It's an ongoing investigation, so I can't answer that."

"Actually, you just did." Layla painted a smile on her face, but it disappeared before she continued. "How is it that his DNA was at the crime scene when he has an alibi? What are we missing?"

Mason silently applauded Layla for not allowing Detective Mansfield's tactics to cause her to doubt herself.

Detective Mansfield released a long breath. "I don't have the answer to that question. We can't be certain his DNA is the missing link to our investigation. Mason knows that. And as you stated, Lackey had an alibi the night of the murder."

Layla nodded, but she didn't let up. "That's the case file version. Give us your version. Surely, you must have had an inkling of what happened, but perhaps you can't prove it. Is it that no one will listen to your theories? No backup?"

Detective Mansfield frowned. Layla's prodding was getting under her skin. These were the moments Mason lived for in the many interviews he'd conducted over the years. Detective Mansfield released another heavy breath. He could almost see her thoughts churning, deciding if now was the time to break her silence. She leaned forward and pushed a manila envelope across the coffee table to Mason.

"Let's just say my theory isn't a priority right now."

Detective Mansfield's merry-go-round answers exasperated him, but Mason gave her his full attention. The small wrinkles in her forehead and near her eyes were evidence of the hardness of her career, but he also saw strength in her features. How much truth could they pull from her?

A far-off look entered her eyes. Her voice was soft, a mismatch from her hardened exterior. "I've been looking into the Lackeys for a couple of years—right after Anthony's first infraction—and even more so after my boss told me to drop the case because my energy was needed elsewhere. I've worked with him for twenty years, and this is the only time he's asked me to let a case go. Something strange is going on, but..." She nodded toward the envelope. "There's only so much digging I can do without the chief finding out."

∞

Layla couldn't be sure about what Mason was thinking right now. Her mind ran rampant with a plethora of thoughts. And everything was confusing. While her confusion could be centered around the fact she was new at this, her gut told her different. Something was off about Detective Mansfield or something fishy was happening down at HPD.

She glanced at Mason, trying to get a read on him without being too obvious. This was her first interview as a journalist, so she wasn't too sure what to believe or if Mason approved of her line of questioning or even if he bought Detective Mansfield's story. Regardless of her doubts, she trusted Mason would stop her or somehow jump in if the conversation needed to go in a different direction.

"Can you tell us what you think may be happening?" Layla pressed.

Detective Mansfield shot her an agitated look, but she answered anyway. "I don't like to speak on anything unless I have facts. He should have told you that." She glared at Mason. "However, the only thing I'm certain of is the chief's relationship with Congresswoman Lackey has clouded his judgment."

Layla allowed Detective Mansfield's comment to sink in. "Are you insinuating that the chief and Congresswoman Lackey are involved in an affair?"

Detective Mansfield smirked. "I'll leave that to you and Mason to piece together."

While she hadn't offered them much more information, Layla believed the detective said enough to give her and Mason something to work with as they continued their research and investigation into the Lackeys.

Mason sat perched on the edge of the sofa as if ready to pounce at any moment, but he hadn't added much to their conversation.

Detective Mansfield sipped her coffee as if her work was complete. "Let me just say this: If I had any indisputable proof that Anthony Lackey murdered anyone, he'd be in jail right now. And those families would have justice."

Layla exchanged looks with Mason. His expression was still unreadable, but she could feel his energy. Frustration raked over him. Detective Mansfield wasn't giving them any helpful information or telling them anything they didn't already know. She scanned the questions on her electronic tablet then lifted her gaze to the detective's. The woman was playing games with her, wasting her time.

"So far, you haven't given us any real information. You suggested you knew we were coming. You've also suggested the chief is covering up Anthony Lackey's wrongdoings because of his extramarital affair with the congresswoman. What information does the chief not want released to the public?" Up until this moment, Layla believed her questions were plain, open, simple, but not enough to pull the truth from the woman.

Detective Mansfield stood and walked over to the balcony doors and peered around as if she expected to see someone. "The truth will get me killed." Her voice was low enough that Layla wasn't sure if she'd heard her correctly. She looked to Mason who wore a similar confused expression with wrinkled brows and frown lines across his forehead.

She spun around to face Layla and Mason. "And the truth is, neither of you should be here. Mason shouldn't have brought you here." Layla stiffened. Weren't those the same words she'd heard in her nightmare?

"What is that supposed to mean?"

"It means that someone is willing to kill to bury the truth, and anyone who stands in the way will get a six-foot-under appointment."

Layla asked what she knew Detective Mansfield wouldn't answer, but she had to do so anyway. "Were you threatened or bribed to keep quiet and look the other way?"

Detective Mansfield didn't answer. Instead, her eyes shifted to the manila envelope on the table in front of Mason and Layla. With her arms folded across her chest, she took measured steps toward them. Her calm demeanor bothered Layla. Maybe it was a situation where misery loved company, not that Layla was miserable, but when she cared about a cause, she preferred everyone to give the same energy. And Detective Mansfield's energy told her that her care meter measured at zero. Mason could obviously sense it, too. He leaped out of his seat.

Layla watched as Detective Mansfield stood unwavering, toe-to-toe with Mason. She glanced up at him. "I told you everything I know."

"Which is nothing."

"It's best that you leave. And as much as you don't want to hear this, Mason, this is one case you need to walk away from. This situation is far more dangerous than you're prepared to handle. Leave it to the authorities to deal with the ballistics and finding the killer—it won't be long before the truth is revealed." She cast her eyes to Layla and back toward the envelope on the table.

"Leave it to them to do nothing." Mason shook his head. "I can't do that. You literally just told us that nothing would be done. You need to decide which side of the truth you want to be on before it's too late."

He reached for Layla's hand, and she accepted his aid helping her stand. "We'll leave for now, but this isn't the last you'll be seeing of us, detective."

Layla slipped her crossbody purse over her shoulder. Detective Mansfield handed her portfolio bag to her, and she stuffed her electronic tablet inside. She followed Mason to the door and turned before she walked out. "Thank you for your time, detective."

"Good luck."

When the detective closed the door and Layla and Mason heard the locks engage, they journeyed back toward his truck in the parking lot. Detective Mansfield's words echoed in her mind. *Good luck.* How could she wish them luck when she hadn't given them anything to go on? Not an ounce of new information for their story. However, she'd learned that nothing was ever wasted. After she and Mason put their heads together, surely, they could pull something from that interview.

It couldn't have been a complete waste of time, could it?

Back inside his vehicle, Layla turned her attention to Mason. "I'm sorry we didn't get the information we hoped we'd get from her. It seems we may be right back where we started."

"I wouldn't be so sure. Check your bag."

Confused, Layla opened her portfolio bag to see the envelope from Detective Mansfield's coffee table stuffed inside. She snapped her head up to see Mason's smiling eyes. Her pulse quickened. Layla didn't know if she should be excited or worried that Mason took the envelope, but one thing was now certain, there was no turning back. Would he really not stop at anything to get a story?

CHAPTER EIGHT

There were questions people already knew the answers to but asked for self-gratification. Then there were questions people knew the answers to but didn't ask because they were afraid to confirm what they knew to be true. The question about the envelope fell somewhere in between. Though Mason seemed pleased, Layla's insides danced to the point she might be sick. Was she an accomplice? Okay, so he didn't kill anyone, but stealing the envelope was still an illegal activity. Even she drew the line somewhere. Should she even look inside the envelope or pretend she knew nothing of its contents?

Calm down and hear his side. You had a hand in helping Langston Brands look good after your sister's murder charges. This is easy.

But seriously? What else was he willing to do? First, an envelope? Next, he'd be blindfolding the woman and shoving her into the backseat of his truck. And Layla wouldn't have a choice but to help because she was in the car with him—basically an accomplice.

Mason's voice cut through her thoughts. "Before you freak out, Detective Mansfield dropped the envelope into your bag."

"Who's freaking out?" Layla asked, willing her voice steady because her thoughts were all over the place.

Mason started the engine and chuckled. He turned down the radio and held her gaze. "Your face. You look like you've seen a ghost or something."

"Why'd she put the envelope in my bag instead of just handing it to one of us?"

"Someone is watching her and possibly us now that we've paid her a visit. Let's not forget what we're dealing with here: A high-profile politician's son could go away for murder. She's already taken steps to keep this under wraps. And Detective Mansfield knows that too, so I trust she knows what she's doing. Plus, if in fact she was bribed or threatened like we suspect, those same people want to keep her quiet, so we'll have to dig deep to get our answers. Buckle up."

Mason backed out of the parking space and navigated toward San Luis Pass while Layla sat there, confused and mentally running through the morning's events.

"Okay, I clearly missed something. School me, teacher. You seem pleased, but while we were inside, I got the feeling you were frustrated and ready to shake answers out of the poor woman."

With one hand on the steering wheel, Mason used the other to help emphasize his points. "Remember how we discussed body language and paying attention to everything a person didn't say?"

Layla nodded. "Yes, I remember."

"Now, take a moment and think back. Did you notice anything about her body language or attitude?"

65

Layla shifted in her seat so that she half-faced Mason. "For one, she seemed too calm for my liking, almost like she didn't care. I thought it bothered you as well."

Mason nodded. "Go on."

"I definitely noticed that she looked around as if she expected someone else to show up, or maybe she believed someone was watching her. Like, when she walked to the balcony and looked out. She was there for quite a while, almost as if she saw someone. That's when she suggested we leave. Oh, and then her eyes. She kept looking at the envelope on the table."

Mason interrupted. "The same envelope in your bag."

Layla looked at it again. "Only, this isn't the same envelope. Same color, but not the same envelope. The one in my bag is bigger. I'm pretty sure the one on her coffee table was an eight by ten. This one is legal sized."

"Perfect." Mason looked over at her and smiled. "You were paying attention. If you recall, the first thing she said was that she wondered how long it would take for me to pay her a visit. When we followed her inside, she drew my attention to the envelope. That's when I knew that not only had she expected me, but she also prepared for me."

"But she also seemed surprised by the home visit."

"And yet she was still prepared."

Again, Layla didn't know whether she should be excited or weirded out about the chain of events. Was there something that Mason wasn't sharing? He was clearly upset with the woman back inside of her condo.

"You had me fooled in there."

"Oh, don't get me wrong. I was upset, but I'm hoping there's something in that envelope that will get me closer to the answers I need. Otherwise, as promised, we will come back."

Layla shifted her attention back to the manila envelope in her bag. As much as Mason wanted answers, why hadn't he asked her to open it? Did he already know what was inside? At this point, she became suspicious of him, too. Something was going on that she didn't know about. Mason had a hidden agenda, and she vowed to find out what it was. What did he know that he hadn't told her? They were supposed to be something like a team.

She removed the envelope from her bag and took her time unsealing it. The envelope wasn't thick but felt heavy, although not heavy enough for her to notice a difference in her bag's weight. After Layla unsealed it, she peered inside before pulling out the contents. She removed the photos first and looked through each one. Some of them from a few months ago. And she knew that because Mason and his father were both in the photos at restaurants, gyms, and political rallies. The man was handsome, even in lounge clothes. She smiled to herself. And then there were recent photos, one as recent as yesterday of her and Mason leaving Goode Seafood Company.

Layla swallowed to moisten her drying throat. Vivid images of what her sisters had gone through in the past few years flashed through her mind. And although she'd never been kidnapped or been on the receiving end of death threats, she couldn't help but wonder if the photo represented that she'd now have to worry about her life being in danger.

Who was watching them? Watching her?

And why?

∞

Whatever was in that photo had shaken Layla. Literally. Her hands trembled.

Though concerned, he had to keep his eyes on the road. But if he needed to, he wouldn't hesitate to pull over. "What's the matter?"

She set her fear-laced eyes on him and flipped the photo so he could see the image. "What the...?"

Mason plucked the photo from her fingers and looked between the image and the road ahead.

"Mason, why would anyone be watching us?"

He handed the photo back to Layla. "Many reasons. Someone is as interested in this investigation as we are, and that doesn't surprise me, but I can't be sure if that's the reason someone is not only watching us, but taking pictures. It's clear that someone is trying to send a message, but it doesn't bother me. I don't think it's a reason to worry. This isn't the first time I've been photographed."

"Is this the first time you've been investigating the congresswoman and her son?"

Mason huffed and cast a glance over at Layla. "You've got a point."

"I've seen a lot in the past few years, Mason. My sisters have both been targets of some crazy people. I'd hate to be next. We need to call the authorities."

"And tell them what? Someone took photos of us? That's not exactly an illegal activity. Plus, we don't know who took the pictures."

"Detective Mansfield should know. How else would she be in possession of them?"

"I'm sorry. You'll have to forgive me if I lack trust in our justice system. Besides, I can handle myself and take care of you, too. And if it makes you feel any better, I have military training and friends who I can call on to help if needed."

"I had no idea you have a military background. Why didn't you say anything before now?"

Mason shrugged. "It hasn't been important until now. I only mention it for your benefit. I've been in the army reserve for the past fifteen years. While on active duty, I served alongside friends who now own their own private security firm. Trust me, we're good."

Recognition filled Layla's eyes. She hiked her eyebrows. "I also know of a private security firm, The Four Kings."

"I'm familiar with them, but why do you know about them?"

She released a heavy sigh and threw her head back against the head rest. "We needed their services a couple of years ago. Plus, my sister, Ava, just married Zack, one of the owners." Something changed in her expression. Worry was what he'd describe with her eyes widening and her slightly parted lips. He could almost see her thoughts churning.

"Hopefully it won't come to us needing to hire bodyguards."

He sure hoped not. Because if they needed private security or any security protection at all, Detective Mansfield and his boss, Simon, were both right—the investigation had become dangerous. But he had no reason to believe anyone wanted to harm him or Layla. A photo didn't prove anything. For all he knew, Detective Mansfield could have hired someone to take that photo to prove she'd been keeping an eye on him.

On the other hand, someone could be lurking in the shadows ready to stop him from figuring out the truth. If these people were willing to harm him, that could only mean this would be one heck of a story. And that thought excited him even more.

"I don't think we'll need to call on The Four Kings." At least not yet.

She twisted her lips as if in deep thought before she finally said, "Okay. I trust you, but if I get the feeling we need to get them involved, I won't hesitate to put in the call."

"I wouldn't expect anything less from you."

And he wouldn't. Mason knew Layla wouldn't compromise her safety for a story. He'd done risky things in the past to get the story he wanted. Layla wasn't at his level of crazy just yet.

Mason nodded toward the envelope. "What else is in there?"

Layla sifted through more photos. "These look like images taken from a murder scene. I wouldn't even know what to look for in them, but since they're in here, the pictures have to be important. I'll put these aside for you to look through later."

She stuffed her hand back inside the envelope and removed pages of what he could only assume were notes, some typewritten, others handwritten. For a while, Layla remained quiet while she read some of the documents.

"Names, dates, notes from her investigation into the congresswoman are all here. Insurance maybe? In the event something happens to her, she wants the truth to get out. I'm a newbie, so I'm just taking guesses here. For example, this note here reads, 'Provided Captain Gritlock evidence. Evidence contained DNA of Anthony Lackey at the scene. When Detective followed up with Captain, Captain said that evidence had been tainted. Report false. Captain said that Congresswoman Lackey wanted this situation to go away ASAP.' That's the end of the note. I think we need to have a talk with Captain Gritlock."

Mason ground his teeth. "I couldn't agree more."

CHAPTER NINE

No more restraints.

The top part of the box she'd been packed inside of was no longer sealed. Light filtered inside.

Layla was finally free.

There weren't any voices. Detective Mansfield was the last person's voice she heard and recognized. Then there was a man's voice. A voice that sounded a lot like Mason's, but she couldn't be certain it was him. And another indistinguishable voice in which Layla couldn't determine if it was a man or woman. The person spoke as if something covered their mouth.

Layla inflated her chest with a big gulp of air and took her time rising out of the box, uncertain of what she'd see when she had a clear view. Her body was stiff from lying in the same position for so long.

She canvassed the area, which looked a lot like the living room in Detective Mansfield's condo. Layla stepped out onto the cold hardwood floors. The wood creaked under her weight. She whipped her head around at the sound to find she was alone in the room. And she was certain there wasn't another living soul nearby because she could feel the emptiness. For a person who lived alone,

Layla normally wouldn't be bothered by the eerie silence, but stepping out of a pine box in the center of someone else's house, dressed in a floor-length white nightgown, was not her idea of perfect peace.

Layla crept through the space into the kitchen where she remembered the detective gazing through the double glass balcony doors. The only thing in sight was the water crashing against the shore. She couldn't even see any other buildings, which she distinctly remembered being nearby.

Who or what could Detective Mansfield have seen that day that made her suggest Layla and Mason leave? Or was that simply all part of her plan?

Layla gave herself a tour of Detective Mansfield's condo. On one hand, she knew she should get out of there and find help, but she also needed to find out why she was there. There had to be a reason someone left her inside of this woman's place, right?

Though she didn't have any doubts about being alone, she still knocked on the first door down the hall once she walked out of the kitchen.

"Hello."

Not expecting a response, she went inside. No bed. No dressers. No wall décor. Nothing. Layla inched toward a set of French doors she assumed led to a restroom. And they did. The restroom was clean, possibly unused, if the empty bedroom was any indication.

Her heart drummed in her ears.

This had to be a scene from one of those crime shows she watched on her favorite streaming service. At any point, she halfway expected someone to appear ready to throw her back inside the pine box for good this time.

Outside of the room, Layla took slow steps down the hall to the next room. She knocked and twisted the knob. "Anybody here?"

Opposite the room she'd just walked out of, this bedroom was decorated in shades of yellow and gray. The comforters on the four-poster bed were disheveled, and the room smelled of expired food and trash. In fact, the stench was so strong, Layla pinched her nose and investigated the source of the stomach-turning smell. She inched around the bed and noticed drops of dried blood stains leading to another set of French doors.

This would probably be the time to run out of there, but she couldn't help herself. Perhaps this was the reason she'd been left here. Or was someone trying to set her up?

Layla held her breath and snatched open the doors. Covered in blood and a swarm of gnats, Detective Mansfield's body was strewn across the bathroom floor.

Oh no.

With a pace ten times as fast as when she'd walked inside the bedroom, Layla fled the scene back into the living room area where she tripped over the pine box.

Layla awakened to sweat-soaked satin sheets and heavy breathing. Everything about that dream seemed real—too real. Sure, she'd had dreams, or rather, nightmares that felt real, but this was different. It was almost as if she'd been transported back into Detective Mansfield's condo to witness she'd been killed.

There was a time in her life when she appreciated having visions because they served her or her family well. Those premonitions were of good fortune, but lately, nothing about her dreams was good. And honestly, she wished she knew what could be done to make them go away. The dreams weren't fun anymore. Fun was when she knew before Crystal and Ava that they'd found their love matches in Marcel and Zack. Fun was when she dreamed her professors would cancel class. Or when she dreamed she'd get the Christmas or birthday present she'd asked for. But this, nightmares of being trapped in a pine box and seeing a dead body, wasn't her idea of fun.

Maybe if she told Mason everything, the nightmares would stop. Wasn't that how the saying went? If you shared your dreams or nightmares with another person, whatever a person experienced in the dream wouldn't come to pass?

Layla yanked the covers off the bed and carried them through her one-story home into the laundry room before going to the master en suite. And as much as she tried, she couldn't shake the heaviness from her mind and body, which weighed on her like an oversized weighted blanket.

The dreams were all too much.

Layla started the shower, and as the steam filled the restroom, she prayed.

Lord, I don't know what to do with these dreams, visions, nightmares, or whatever they may be. Never in my life have I encountered anything like this, and I don't know what to do about them. But above all else, I believe in purpose, and I know that You have established purpose in this situation. So, please, show me what You want me to do and give me relief. I trust that You will lead me in the path I should go. In Jesus' name. Amen.

After her shower, Layla made up her mind. She'd tell Mason everything. About every single dream. And she whispered another prayer that he would understand and possibly be the person to help her figure things out.

And her third prayer that morning was hoping what she saw about Detective Mansfield wasn't literal. Could it be a sign that she and Mason needed to warn her? But even she wouldn't believe someone who came to her with a warning because of a dream they'd had.

Layla dressed and called Mason before she gathered all of her things to leave for work. The sooner she got her sleeping life off her chest, the better off she'd be.

Mason answered on the first ring. "Morning. I came into the office early. Just got out of a meeting with Simon. I have some news for you, and it's best I share it in person."

Layla's heart raced. Had he uncovered information that would help bring their investigation to a close sooner than they'd planned? Was there something in the documents they'd retrieved from Detective Mansfield that brought about this news? She wasn't sure if she should be excited or worried about whatever Mason had to tell her.

Her hands trembled as she grabbed her keys, crossbody purse, and portfolio bag. If Mason's news was good, he would have come on out with it as opposed to making her wait. Layla swallowed to moisten her drying throat. Bad news was coming. She could feel it, much like she could feel the heaviness from the death she'd witnessed in her REM sleep.

"Okay." Layla stressed the second syllable much longer than needed. "I'm on my way because I have something I need to share with you, too."

"Drive safely. I'll be waiting."

"Thanks."

Layla locked up her house. She tossed her belongings in the passenger's seat of her car before claiming her space behind the steering wheel. The fight to keep positive thoughts was difficult when her belly churned the same way it always did when she suspected something bad was about to happen. She prayed today would be an exception, but her gut was never wrong.

∞

Mason repeatedly replayed the conversation he'd just had with Simon in his head. Was the incident his fault? Or would it have happened even if he and Layla didn't pay Detective Mansfield a visit? Did she know what was coming? Was that the reason she'd given him every piece of information she had on the congresswoman?

His temples throbbed.

And it wasn't as if Mason hadn't covered at least forty investigations before now, from politics, murders, and even drug busts, but none of them affected him like this current assignment. To his knowledge, no one had wound up dead either.

Mason steepled his fingers, rested his forehead against them, and silently prayed for mental strength and direction in this investigation. Though the situation was unfortunate, he couldn't stop now. And after he shared the news with Layla, he wouldn't hold her decision against her if she chose to walk away. In fact, he expected her to request another mentor. It didn't matter that they worked well together or that he was fond of her. Her safety came first. And if their presence was what caused the stir in Detective Mansfield's condo, he could only imagine what would come next. He could handle himself and her, but he preferred that she had no parts in this investigation any longer.

He jumped out of his seat and marched back into Simon's office. His breathing was heavy enough to see the exaggerated rise and fall of his chest. "Reassign Layla."

Simon squinted and stared him in the eyes, no doubt trying to read him. He threaded his arms across his chest and leaned back in his seat. "Why? I thought you two were getting along well."

"Because, as you insinuated in the beginning, this could get dangerous, and I don't want her anywhere near this investigation. If what happened to Detective Mansfield is my fault, then who's to say that whoever did this won't come after her—I mean us—next."

Recognition filled Simon's eyes. Yes, Mason cared about Layla far more than he should, and thankfully, Simon didn't call him on it. Mason didn't have time to get into a discussion about his emotions right now, nor did he want to. He had to protect Layla, and he needed Simon on his side. It was better if Simon redirected her than for Mason to suggest she work with someone else. As far as he was concerned, she could handle being on her own anyway.

Simon hunched over his desk and clasped his hands together. "Okay, but with knowing how potentially dangerous this investigation is, I don't want you going about it alone. Who do you have in mind to replace Layla?"

"Replace me?"

Mason whipped his head around at the sound of Layla's shrieking voice. Her mouth was slightly ajar, and her eyes wide. He could see the hurt and disappointment in her eyes, which made his chest physically ache.

Without shifting his focus from her, he said, "Excuse me, Simon. Give me a minute while I talk to Layla." He gestured toward their cubicle area. No matter what he said to her in the next few minutes or how he said it, he'd already caused a rift in their working relationship and anything personal that may have developed as well. "Please join me so I can tell you what this is about."

He could tell by the squint in her eyes and the puff in her chest that she wrestled with maintaining a professional response. After several seconds passed, her chest deflated. She spun on her heels, leaving him to scramble to catch up with her. All Mason could think was how he'd get his point across in a way to help her understand his position.

Back at her desk, Layla sat with her legs crossed at the knee and her arms folded across her chest. Her defiant chin and hard eyes challenged him. Even though his intent was to keep her safe, she made him feel like he'd done something wrong. And all he wanted was to do something—anything—that would bring back the smile that lit up his heart.

Mason pulled his seat into her cubicle and sat across from her. He took a deep breath. His heart didn't have a voice in this situation. He needed her to step aside this time.

Layla still hadn't spoken again. Instead, she cocked her head to one side and lifted an impatient eyebrow. Mason was certain that she'd already made up her mind not to agree with anything he said. But he had to try anyway, although ultimately the decision was up to her and Simon.

"I don't know how much you heard of me and Simon's conversation, but it isn't what you think."

"How is it not what I think? We make a great team so why are you trying to get rid of me?"

"I'm trying to protect you, Layla. Why can't you see that? This investigation is becoming dangerous. I don't want you to get hurt. You didn't sign up for this."

"You think I'm not aware of the risks? Did we also not discuss getting The Four Kings involved if it came to that?"

"Detective Mansfield is dead."

Layla drew her hands to her face, covering her nose and mouth. Tears puddled in her eyes, yet they didn't fall. She rocked back and forth in her seat. Once she blinked, a stream of tears slid down her cheeks, and her shoulders shook.

Mason leaped out of his seat to grab a box of tissues from a nearby file cabinet, returned, and handed a few pieces to Layla. He wasn't the best person to deal with emotional matters, so he didn't know how to respond to seeing how the news affected her. He considered hugging her, but couldn't be certain if that was too much.

However, when her tears didn't stop, he tossed aside professional courtesy and allowed his emotions to reign. Mason pulled her to her feet, wrapped his arms around her, and squeezed. He held her until she whispered, "This is my fault, Mason."

Confused, he loosened the embrace, took a step back, and searched her eyes for understanding. "There's no way this is your fault. This is my doing. If we hadn't gone out there, I think she'd still be alive. Whoever did this wants to send a message for us to end our investigation. I don't intend to walk away, and I don't think it's fair to drag you into this. You're just starting out. You don't need this drama."

Layla claimed her seat. "You don't understand, Mason. This is my fault. I knew something would happen. I felt it in my spirit. In fact, I had a dream about her death last night, which is why I called you this morning. That's what I wanted to talk to you about. It felt so real, like I was transported in time or something."

Mason eased back into his seat. Confusion clouded his thoughts. What was he to make of what Layla revealed? Was she some type of fortune teller or something? He'd never believed in anyone being able to tell the future. "So, do you have dreams like this all the time or what? Help me understand."

Layla rolled the crumpled tissues between her fingers. "I typically have these visions sometimes about my family. Like, I knew my sisters had found their husbands before they did. I've seen certain things happen in my family before they took place. I dream about an event, and then it happens."

"Hmmm."

Layla looked off into the distance as if she could see the events unfolding in front of her. "The night before we went to visit her, I had a dream something would happen, but it wasn't clear. I was trapped in this pine box, and—"

"Trapped in a pine box? Like a coffin?"

She nodded.

If she dreamed about an event before it happened, being locked in a coffin was even more reason why she should no longer assist him with his investigation into the congresswoman. What if that situation came to pass? Yet, he couldn't use her dreams as a basis to go to Simon and request someone else mentor her. Even Simon would think he'd lost his mind. They made decisions based off data and facts, not dreams.

"I heard her say that you shouldn't have brought me there."

Mason interjected. "The same thing she said while we were in her condo, which is why you had that look on your face—a little more troubled and bothered about her comment than I thought you should have been. I was confused then, but I understand now. Layla, I think your dreams are warning you to take a step back."

"Are you telling me that this is the only dangerous investigation that I'll ever encounter?"

He couldn't promise that, although he'd never known anyone to be murdered during one of his investigations.

"Even though I'd like to believe this is a one-off situation, I cannot give you any assurance that it isn't."

"Then I stay."

CHAPTER TEN

As displeased as Layla was with Mason, she couldn't blame him for his way of thinking. If she sat in his seat and the situation were reversed, she'd also suggest he remove himself from the investigation. And there was a small part of her that wanted to do so, albeit a very small part, but she couldn't give in. Not now. She accepted this position knowing that she could possibly find herself in dangerous situations. But in the deep recesses of her heart, she didn't truly believe that something bad would happen to her. She leaned toward the idea that her dreams were meant to serve her well in this investigation, no matter how scary they'd been lately.

She and Mason held each other's gaze as if to see who would blink or back down first. Layla fully intended to stay. Mason had to figure out how to deal with the realization.

He huffed and shook his head. That was his way of relenting. Mason didn't have the power to fire her so he might as well accept her decision so they could work together to figure this thing out and get their story.

"I can't believe you'd choose to stay after what you shared with me about your dreams. Not walking away from this is insane."

"Not any more insane than what you're doing." Tension eased out of her body. Her muscles softened. Telling Mason about her dreams was supposed to shock him or make him believe she was crazy. Instead, he took the news well. At least that's what Layla assumed. He didn't look at her like she'd grown a third eye, laugh at her, or even tell her she was out of her mind.

He pressed his forefinger into his chest. "I have to do this. This is my story—a story I've been working on for months. You, on the other hand, can and should walk away."

Layla cracked her knuckles, giving herself a reason not to maintain eye contact. "So, you don't think it's weird that I've been having these dreams? You trust them? Because I'm not entirely sure what to do about them."

Mason took one of her hands in his. Her skin warmed from his touch. Her heart drummed faster, a response she hadn't expected from the connection. She focused on his hands for several seconds, almost willing the emotions to pass. They didn't. Mason gently tugged her fingers to draw her attention to him.

"I don't completely understand what's going on with your dreams, but I do trust you. And based on what you've told me and what I've seen, something is going on here, and it could be that your dreams are trying to tell you something. And I don't have to say what I think they mean again, do I?"

Layla squeezed his hand. "You don't, but I appreciate your concern."

"Taking your safety into account is easy. If anything happens to you, I'd find it hard to forgive myself."

"Then let's stick with the plan to call The Four Kings if things get crazy."

Mason nodded. His hands remained clasped around hers. They were having a moment, weren't they? Layla's heartbeat escalated even more at the thought.

Simon's voice carried into the area before he appeared. They unlinked hands and reverted to a professional distance when he made it to their cubicle area.

Simon folded his arms across his chest. A smirk framed the corner of his lips like he knew the answer to his question before he asked it. "Do you two have a decision about how you'd like to proceed?"

Layla didn't give Mason a chance to respond. "Yes. I want Mason to remain as my mentor, and I'll continue assisting him in his current investigation." She shifted her attention to Mason and added, "As planned."

Whatever conversation Simon and Mason had before she arrived must have caused his hesitation because Simon didn't seem to take her word for it until Mason confirmed her statement. Simon looked to Mason. They'd known each other long enough so that it was clear they were having a silent discussion with their eyes.

Mason nodded. "We're good."

Silence passed between the trio while Simon looked between the two of them. Layla wondered if he knew what she sensed—something was happening between her and Mason. What exactly, she couldn't identify. And she didn't want to spend time attempting to decipher what was going on in Mason's head.

"Then the situation is settled. I don't need to find you another mentor, and you'll continue keeping any eye on him for me. I'll be waiting for updates."

Mason stood and shook Simon's hand. When Simon left, Mason reached for her hand to help her stand. "It's time to pay the police chief a visit."

With the recent death of Detective Mansfield, now was probably as good of a time as any. Layla smiled. "I was thinking the same thing."

∞

Mason's head flooded with a plethora of thoughts. The idea that Layla saw what happened to Detective Mansfield before it happened or while it happened bothered him. Why wasn't she as concerned about her safety as he was? Had she seen something else in her dreams or nightmares or whatever she wanted to call them, that she did not disclose to him? And knowing this part of her also made him wonder if he could trust her. How was he supposed to feel and respond in such a situation? And how did a person even begin to have a conversation about such things?

He glanced over at her riding in the passenger seat. She'd been quiet since they left the office. Nature and the cloudy skies captured her attention on their drive to the police station. Mason didn't speak much either. He'd been processing what she shared with him and the fact that Detective Mansfield was killed last night. Mason assumed she was doing the same.

When he parked in a garage down the street from the police station, Mason cut his engine and shifted in his seat to face her, one arm on the steering wheel. "Are you sure you're alright?"

She turned to him as if his voice startled her. "Oh, yeah, I'm fine. I guess I'm just hoping that this doesn't become a situation where everyone we talk to ends up dead."

"What?"

"C'mon. Don't tell me the thought hasn't crossed your mind."

Mason blew a stream of air. "Briefly, but the idea of that happening is too far-fetched. Offing the police chief will be a stretch. I've got to warn you, though. Chief doesn't like me much. We've had many run-ins over the years because I question him when no one else will. Perhaps he'll play nice today because you're here, but my expectations are low."

Layla released her seatbelt. "Any theories you want to toss around before we go in?"

Mason rubbed his chin and thought for a moment. "Other than the fact that he's covering for Congresswoman Lackey and her son? That part is clear. I just need to know why."

"Maybe she has some dirt on him. From what I know, that's the biggest reason he'd cover for them. He's done something she knows about, and she threatened to expose him if her son was charged for murder."

Mason agreed, but that scenario was too well put together for his liking. Sounded simple, but in his experience, simple was rarely the answer. This cover-up was likely more complicated, more convoluted. Or maybe that was his hope—that whatever Congresswoman Lackey and the police chief were burying had to be big. But Mason's job was to bust up their secret and expose the truth. Nothing was more important.

"I like the way you think, but that's way too easy. He would never admit his wrongdoing if that's the case because he'd likely lose his career if the word got out."

"Of course not. But he might say more to me than he would to you since you two have history. And my dad plays golf with him from time to time so I'm sure I have more favor with him. Plus, I don't mind poking the bear and asking the tough questions. Are you okay with me leading the interview?"

He forced back a smile. Her enthusiasm matched his. He also had personal reasons to seek justice from the chief because Mason believed the man knew more about the explosion that killed his father than what the Fire Investigator made public. It wasn't a secret the chief and Fire Investigator knew each other well. A secret between the two wasn't far-fetched. And although this wasn't Layla's case, and she didn't have personal reasons to seek justice from the chief as he did, her eagerness made him like her a little bit more.

"Actually, I'd prefer you to handle the questioning. Like I said, he doesn't like me. And it seems you may already have a better relationship with him than I do." Mason rested against the seat. "So, what's your first question?"

Layla gave the sort of smile that bordered on mischievousness, and he liked it. She shrugged. "I'm going straight for the kill because he's likely not going to give us much time. I'll preface my question by stating we talked to Detective Mansfield before asking him to give me the reason why he covered up Anthony Lackey's crimes."

Mason fist bumped her. "I don't have to teach you anything. You're a natural."

Layla beamed. "Thanks, but I'm sure there's plenty for me to learn. I need your help to work through this. I know he won't tell me much, if anything, but I'm hoping he'll be upset enough to say something that will help. That way, we can pair that information with the documents we have from Detective Mansfield. And I wouldn't dare tell him that we have physical proof that he didn't actively pursue the case like he should have. For all we know, that could be why Detective Mansfield is dead."

Mason clapped. "Precisely. Let's go get a partial answer."

Layla chuckled and grabbed her purse. Mason hopped out of his vehicle and rounded the truck to open the door for her. Side by side, they purposefully strode out of the parking garage toward the entrance of the Houston Police Department in the downtown Edward E. Thomas building. Mason couldn't count the number of times on both of his hands and feet that he'd been proverbially kicked out of the building. Hopefully, today would tell a different story.

A couple of officers congregated outside the entrance in full uniform. Houstonians who likely worked downtown walked by with five-dollar cups of coffee in their hands chatting with seemingly no cares in the world. Mason and Layla, on the other hand, had enough cares for all of them.

Mason nodded his greeting to the officers and walked a few steps ahead to open the door for Layla. Once inside, he led her to the clerk's desk. The older redhead looked at him and shook her head.

"Not here to cause trouble, Ms. Strawder. Just need to spend a few minutes with the chief."

She looked from him to Layla. "You know he doesn't want to see you, right?"

"I figured as much, but could you see if you can get Ms. Langston face time with him?"

She huffed and shook her head before she nodded and lifted the receiver. When she spoke, she kept her eyes on Mason the entire time. Her voice was quiet, so he couldn't hear what she said. Although, he could only imagine what was being said about him through the line.

"Have a seat. He'll be out in a few minutes."

Layla and Mason found two adjacent seats in the lobby and waited.

An hour later, Chief Gritlock strolled into the lobby holding a stainless-steel coffee mug. He squinted when he locked eyes with Mason.

Mason held up surrendered palms and stood. "I'll be on my best behavior today. I'm only here to accompany Ms. Langston. We only want a few minutes of your time."

He grunted, turned on his heel, and waved them over. "Follow me."

Chief Gritlock gestured in front of him. "Ms. Langston, nice to meet you. My office is the first door to the right after you make the second left."

When Layla walked ahead of them, Chief Gritlock spoke so that only Mason could hear. "Any trouble out of you today, and I'll toss you behind these bars."

CHAPTER ELEVEN

L ayla wasn't sure why Chief Gritlock would take the meeting with her and Mason when his grunts led her to believe he didn't want to do so. She led the way to his office, based on his directional instructions. The pungent smell in the building made her sick to her stomach. Last time she was in a police station, she was there to check on the wellbeing of her oldest sister, Crystal. All those memories rushed back, and they weren't pleasant. She would happily allow Mason to do precinct visits alone in the future.

When she arrived at the chief's office, she stood to the right of the door and waited for him to invite her and Mason inside.

Chief Gritlock walked into his office and called over his shoulder, "Come on in and have a seat."

Layla perched on the edge of the chair. Though the chief's office didn't smell as bad as the rest of the building she'd walked through, the scent lingered in her mind. And as far as she was concerned, his office held the residue of the stench.

The man was probably six-and-a-half feet tall. His towering presence wasn't intimidating, however. His light brown orbs seemed softer than the hard exterior he wanted to portray, while his mahogany skin held its share of wrinkles. And given he'd played

93

golf with her father for quite some time, she could guess his age. He was knocking on the door of retirement.

"Ms. Langston, as in daughter of my golf buddy, Lamont Langston?"

"That would be me."

He grunted. "I hope you aren't here to cause trouble like your friend there." He shifted his attention to Mason. "I mean it. I'll throw you in jail today if I have to."

Layla shot Mason a glance. What had she missed?

Mason held both palms in the air and gestured toward Layla.

"No, sir. No trouble at all. I just have a few questions for you. We're working on the story behind Anthony Lackey's DNA left at a crime scene, yet he wasn't charged with the crime. Anthony Lackey as in Congresswoman Lackey's son." She waited for acknowledgement to go ahead. He nodded. "I met with Detective Mansfield two days ago."

Chief Gritlock stiffened in his seat, and though he tried to hide it, Layla saw the shock in his face. He hiked an eyebrow. "Go on," he said, his voice steady.

"Based on my conversation with her, it seems HPD has a history in burying facts in Anthony Lackey's crimes—and that's plural. Why hasn't your office arrested him?"

The chief smoothed his hand along the front of his shirt over his protruding belly and leaned forward, shifting his weight on the desk. "Anthony Lackey was cleared because the DNA evidence was a dead end. He had an alibi for that evening."

"So, we've been told, but—"

Chief Gritlock cut her off. "I trust my detectives to explore any and all leads to solve their cases.

Mason piped in. "Just like you trusted the word of the Fire Investigator about the explosion that killed my father? You trust everyone around you, Chief?"

He huffed and squinted his eyes at Mason. "I have no reason to believe he didn't do his job well."

Mason's nostrils flared, and his chest heaved. While upset, he didn't have a basis for his belief that something was amiss in the investigation other than his gut and the fact he'd had months to think about the facts.

Layla piggybacked off Mason's question, though off topic of why they were visiting the chief. Voicing his opinion would only make it appear like his grief clouded his judgement, but she had no personal stake in the matter. "Is there reason to believe the Fire Investigator's report isn't accurate? Is it possible the explosion was intentional, and Mr. Sterling was targeted?"

When the chief didn't respond, scrunched his eyebrows, and curled his lips in anger, she pressed.

"And what about Detective Mansfield? Is her death somehow related?"

"Get out."

Layla pressed more. "Chief, how is the congresswoman involved? Is she paying you to look the other way or bribing you? Did she have anything to do with that explosion? What have you done—"

"This meeting is over, Ms. Langston. Please leave. And if I see you around here again, I'll toss you in a cell next to your partner here."

Not in the least bit satisfied, Layla stood anyway. So did Mason. She'd tried not to allow the chief's words to affect her, so she hoped her facial expressions got the message. From the moment the chief opened his mouth, she knew he wouldn't tell her anything that would help their story. Why would he? But the interview was fun and good practice.

"Does Lamont know this is what you're up to these days?"

"Oh, I'm sure he's proud," Layla said before walking out of his office.

When they were outside of the precinct and back on the sidewalk of downtown Houston, Mason turned to her, never breaking stride. "Where have you been all my life?"

Layla burst into laughter. Mason joined. "I'm so serious. Do you know how long it took me to get threats like that from Chief Gritlock? And here you are getting kicked out during your first interview."

She shrugged. "Takes a special person to get kicked out of someone's office, huh? I knew we wouldn't get anything from him, but pressing his buttons was fun. Whatever the situation, the chief is on someone's payroll, and it's not just the City of Houston. When we get all the answers we need, I've got a feeling that we're going to uncover a lot of dirt. And folks in high places are about to come tumbling down."

"That's the kind of fight I'm looking for."

Layla fist bumped him. "Bringing accountability one story at a time."

Though she was a grown woman, she needed to talk to her father before the chief did. She was a journalist now with the duty and responsibility to find and expose the truth, and she didn't need anyone interfering, especially not her father. There was no telling how the chief would spin their meeting, and as a result, how her father would try to help.

"Absolutely."

Layla and Mason returned to the office where she excused herself to make the phone call to her father. She didn't want to bring him or any of her family into this, but when the chief brought her father's name up in conversation, she knew he'd call and tattle, hoping her father would put her in her place. But she had news for Chief Gritlock: She was exactly where she needed to be. And she didn't care who liked it.

Layla escaped into one of the mother's rooms where she'd have complete privacy and didn't have to worry about anyone barging in. She tapped the call icon under her father's contact card. While the phone rang, she paced the carpet in the small space and waited for him to answer.

"Dad, hey. How are you?"

"Doing just fine. How are things at *The Houston Exposure*?"

And that's when she knew he'd already talked to Chief Gritlock. Her father never asked about work first, even when she worked at Langston Brands.

"It's good. Seems I might have a long road ahead of me on the story I'm assisting my mentor with."

"I heard. Calvin just called me, said you and Mason Sterling were stirring up trouble."

Her father had never been one to believe outsiders over his family, but she still had to ask. "You don't believe that do you?"

"No, but I know you, and I want you to be careful out there. Now, don't get me wrong. I know you have a job to do, but you should know that I care about your safety. Who is this Mason fella?"

"He's training me. He and the chief don't have a good relationship, so it's not surprising that Chief Gritlock called you. Not stirring up trouble, only trying to find answers about this politician's son's involvement in recent crimes." And while she didn't mention it to her father, there was also the possibility she'd find out if there was more to the explosion that killed Walter Sterling. Mason's mentioning of the incident back in Chief Gritlock's office had her more curious.

"Calvin mentioned that, too. Said *The Houston Exposure* should spend their resources investigating something else."

Layla continued to pace the floor. She kept her voice low just in case, though she doubted anyone could hear her. "If you ask me, I think he knows what the congresswoman has been up to and he's covering it up."

"That's a huge accusation. Don't say things like that unless you can back it up."

"Oh, that's exactly what I plan to do."

Her dad's stern voice came through the line. She could only imagine the look on his face. "Layla, you're a grown woman, so I can't tell you what to do, but I will say this. You're treading on dangerous territory by questioning the chief of police and accusing him of knowing the truth and not acting on it. I don't like this and won't hesitate to get Zack and his brothers involved."

"Dad, if it comes to that, I'll call The Four Kings myself. Try not to worry. I'll be fine. I trust Mason, and we have each other's backs."

"I mean it. I don't know this Mason any more than I know how to solve a Rubik's Cube, and I will get involved if it means keeping you out of harm's way."

"I know that, Dad, but don't worry."

After a few more rounds of him threatening to call The Four Kings and trying his best at encouraging Layla to request another mentor, she ended the call. They'd agree to disagree. She was invested in this story now—for herself and for Mason.

Chief Gritlock had done nothing more than make himself look even guiltier by calling her father. If he thought one phone call to Daddy would make her back off, he'd have to try harder than that. All he did was throw a lit match on her lighter fluid–soaked charcoals—he'd see her again.

∞

Layla amazed Mason every step of their investigative way. When she stepped away to make a personal phone call, he sat in his cubicle and waited for her return. His thoughts drifted back to their meeting with the chief. He admired the way she held her ground and didn't allow the man to intimidate her. Of course, they weren't going to learn anything new from Chief Gritlock, but Mason wanted to send a clear message—they were watching and suspicious of him. And soon enough, all of Houston would know the chief had a hand in covering up Congresswoman Lackey's and her son's crimes.

Mason gave Layla his full attention when she arrived back in her cubicle. He shifted his seat to face her. Layla beamed, and he couldn't help but return the smile.

She sat and faced him as well. "Next steps?"

Mason shouldn't get in her business, but that's what he did best. "How'd the conversation with your dad go?"

Her eyebrows shot up. "How'd you know I was talking to my dad?"

"It's obvious. Chief mentioned him on our way out of his office, and from what you've shared with me about your family, you all seem close. It's not surprising. The man probably called your father before you did."

She teased, "Curiosity getting the best of you, I see. But you can probably imagine how the conversation went. He's concerned with my safety, but I assured him we're fine."

"And he bought it?"

Layla frowned and pursed her lips. "What do you mean? I am fine, and I'm careful."

Mason toyed with the pen in his hand. "You know exactly what I'm talking about. The dream. Detective Mansfield. And how this could all change course without warning. Your father knows what he's talking about. And now that the chief knows we're asking questions, he'll be watching us, too. Detective Mansfield is dead, Layla. And to the murderers, our lives may not be worth anything to them either."

"Are you going to try to talk me out of this investigation after every interview? Because if you are, you're wasting your time and your breath when we could use that energy to be more productive."

Mason tossed his head back and released a long stream of air. He didn't want Layla off the assignment, but he had to give her an out, just in case. In fact, his preference was to keep her in his sight at all times. He couldn't let anyone harm her because he wasn't willing to let his anger and disappointment in the justice system slide.

He changed the subject. "Did you get that meeting scheduled with the DA?"

Layla pulled out her phone and the screen illuminated. "Not yet. I was waiting for him to call me back. I could just call my sister, but wanted to keep this professional and approach him as the DA and not my brother-in-law. I don't want to get her involved if I didn't have to."

Mason waved the envelope they'd received from Detective Mansfield. "Good, because we need to prepare for our meeting with him. Let's spend some time going through the documents we got from Detective Mansfield. I'd like to have as much information as possible before we go to the DA."

"Sounds good. And what about Anthony Lackey? When are we going to the hospital to pay him a visit?"

"After we go through these documents. Maybe there's something in here that will make both our interview with him and our meeting with the DA more productive."

Layla nodded. "Okay, then. Let's see what we've got."

When Mason removed the contents from the envelope, a thumb drive fell on his desk. He held it up and waved it in the air. "Let's just hope it's not password protected."

Mason shoved the drive into his laptop and slid over to Layla's cubicle. She rolled her chair to the left to make room for him. The space was just enough for the two of them, but he'd never mind being close to her. Once his computer ran its virus scan, Mason opened the file labeled *Congresswoman Melissa Lackey*. Hundreds of files, including photos, Word documents, and databases were there.

Layla leaned in closer and touched his screen, pointing at the file labeled *Crime Scene Detail*. "Wow."

Inside the folder were photos of blood on the concrete where the victim laid before the paramedics hoisted him onto the gurney. Blood on the victim's knuckles. And photos of empty bullet casings scattered on the ground.

Mason continued clicking through photos. They appeared to be duplicates, some of them more magnified than others. When he finished looking through the pictures, he turned to Layla. "Did anything catch your eye in the photos?"

She shook her head. "Nothing other than what I would expect to see in crime scene photos. Am I missing something?"

Mason clicked back to one of the photos with splatters of blood on the concrete. "I'm not sure. And without DNA, I can't be certain if what I'm thinking is correct. But do you see here," he pointed at the screen, "and here," he clicked and pointed at another photo. "These are two different areas of the concrete. And if you think about it logically, once the victim was shot, he likely would have gone down in this area," he said, pointing to the photo that had the most blood. "So where did this blood come from? Could there have been a third person?"

"Apparently the police think so, which is why Anthony Lackey hasn't been arrested."

Layla hovered her fingers over his keyboard. "Do you mind?"

"Go ahead."

She clicked and typed. "Let's create a separate folder for items that need a closer look and that would probably make sense once we put everything together." She moved a couple of the photos to that folder. When she finished, she sat back in her seat.

"Thanks, but you know I could've done that, right?"

She shrugged and tilted her head. "I have to pull my weight around here, don't you think?"

Mason chuckled. "Yeah, you're right."

"Do you think Detective Mansfield was being strategic when she gave us all these documents? What I mean by that is, do you think this is just an investigation dump of information, or is everything here important and all critical to helping us piece this story together?"

"In a perfect world, we'd only have what we need, but in this case, I think she gave us everything she had. Since she was somehow restricted from doing her job, I believe it's left up to me—well, us—to find the missing links."

Layla pointed at the screen. "Well, okay then. Let's take a look at her interview notes."

Mason double clicked the folder to open the file labeled *Interviews.*

"Let's start with Anthony Lackey. It's his DNA at the scene. I wonder what else Detective Mansfield had to say about him during the course of her investigation. Remember those handwritten notes in that folder?" Layla pointed to the legal-sized envelope on his desk. "She thought he was guilty."

Mason opened the computer file. "Right. I'm hoping to understand what the chief saw and why he believes the DNA or crime scene was tainted."

"Right."

Mason and Layla sat in silence while he scrolled through page after page, reading Detective Mansfield's interview notes with Anthony Lackey. Apparently, he was at some club with his brother. Too convenient, if you asked Mason. Both of them would share the same DNA. And for them both to be at a club the night of the murder in question didn't gel with him.

Did Detective Mansfield even check video footage at the club that night?

Mason continued scrolling.

She had notes of viewing video footage, but she questioned the time stamp. However, nothing came of that because the chief told her she was wasting resources. And then there was the corroboration of their mother, who said they were at her home during the time of the murder, before they left for the night club.

"This is insane," Layla blurted out. "I'm not a cop, and I don't believe this murder was thoroughly investigated."

"Yeah, me either." Mason stood. "Let's take a break at Memorial Hermann in the Texas Medical Center. Maybe Anthony Lackey can help us fill in the gaps."

CHAPTER TWELVE

Layla had to figure out a way to talk Mason into letting her handle the Anthony Lackey interview alone. Ever since Mason mentioned the explosion in Chief Gritlock's office, she wondered if it were possible for Congresswoman Lackey to have ties to the explosion that caused Mr. Sterling's demise. Could it be possible that Mr. Sterling was targeted? When she blurted the question out to Chief Gritlock, she hadn't thought about the possibility. But what if the explosion wasn't an accident? That is what Mason suggested, right?

With determined strides, they walked out of the building to the parking garage. Mason always assigned himself the task of driving them around. When they made it to his Dodge Ram, he thrust his arm in front of her to halt her tracks, while he stepped closer and circled the vehicle.

"Not one, but four flat tires."

Layla inched closer and peered at the passenger's side back tire. "You don't suppose this has anything to do with our investigation, do you?"

"I'd be lying if I said no. If this were random, my vehicle wouldn't be the only one with damage." Mason muttered something she couldn't understand, but could guess at the expletive. He pulled out his phone and called a tow truck.

When he finished his call, she asked, "Are you going to file a police report?"

Mason circled his truck and snapped photos of each tire. "I can imagine how that will go. They'll find no evidence and not do anything about the situation. It'll be a waste of my time and theirs."

Layla nodded, but didn't respond. Mason's trust in law enforcement wasn't high right now. Besides, she couldn't think of what they'd do to help this situation. And given the fact they saw Chief Gritlock recently, she couldn't be certain if he had something to do with this. She didn't get any positive vibes during their meeting with him, so she questioned his loyalty to protect and serve these days.

They waited twenty minutes for the tow truck driver to arrive and another fifteen minutes for him to collect Mason's information and hitch the vehicle onto the tow.

"Thank goodness my tires are fine so that means I'll be our driver for today." She led him over to her red two-door coupe. "Hop in. I promise to take it easy."

Mason chuckled as he opened the driver's side door for her. Once she was safely inside, he rounded the car and climbed into the passenger's seat. He clicked on his seatbelt and double-checked that it fastened, then he tugged at the handle near the window.

"What is all this about? I'm a great driver."

Mason chuckled again. "I never said you weren't. Just checking that I have something to hold on to, just in case. Plus, people who are great drivers don't have to say so."

Layla bubbled in laughter. "I haven't given you any reason to believe that I'm a reckless driver. I've got you." She turned the engine and shifted the gear into reverse.

The realization of what happened to Mason's vehicle settled in. Would someone flatten her tires too or do something worse to persuade them to drop the story? An aching feeling weighed in the pit of her belly. She cast a casual glance toward Mason. No doubt he wondered the same thing, but there was nothing anyone could do to stop him.

She kept her voice calm and soothing, almost like that of a late-night radio deejay. "Has anything like this ever happened to you while investigating a story?"

"I've received threatening phone calls, e-mails, and letters in the office, but nothing physical. No one has ever touched my personal property. And to be transparent with you, Layla, this is too coincidental that this happens after we talked to Chief Gritlock. If he thinks slashed tires will stop me, then he doesn't know me at all. If he wants to stop me, he'll have to kill me first."

Layla's breath caught. "Don't say things like that."

"Why not, if I mean it? I've been honest with you since we started working together. I won't stop until I get the answers I need. At any point, you can walk away, and I won't be offended. I don't want any harm to come to you because of me."

Visions of Mason covered in blood on a slab of concrete danced through her mind. Horrible thoughts she wouldn't want to happen to him.

Couldn't let that happen to him.

At the next opportunity, she pulled to the side of the road into a gas station parking lot a couple of streets before her turn into their destination at Memorial Hermann hospital. Layla shifted her gear into park and turned to him.

"What's going on?" He leaned over and looked at her dashboard. She assumed he checked her gas gauge.

"We need to talk."

"What's on your mind?"

Layla inhaled enough air to fill her chest, then released the air slowly. She licked her lips. "I'm just going to shoot straight. I don't think you need to go into that hospital room."

He parted his lips, but before he could speak, she raised her palm to stop him. He frowned, but nodded for her to continue.

"Just hear me out. First, you may not want to admit it, but your emotions are all over the place. Second, if Chief Gritlock is working with the congresswoman, then he's likely already talked to her, which means her and her family could possibly be expecting us, but more so you than me. If Anthony Lackey is going to say anything, chances are he'll speak to me before you. I'm much less threatening."

Mason relaxed in his seat with his right arm propped on the door. He massaged his chin. "You aren't wrong, but you can't expect me to sit here and do nothing."

Layla reached across the center console and covered his hands with hers. "But you are doing something. You're trusting me to flex my skills, and you're gathering your composure. Someone just slashed your tires, Mason. You're ticked off."

"Okay. I'll agree to allowing you to handle the interview, if—"

"No," she cut him off. "Not just handling the interview. You shouldn't even be in the room. If Congresswoman Lackey is working with the chief like we suspect, then he's already talked to her about our visit, and they'd be on high alert. It's obvious he doesn't like you. You're probably on the 'do not enter' list."

"And you're not?"

"I'm a newbie so it's unlikely. He probably thinks a call to my dad put me in my place."

Mason chuckled and held her gaze for several seconds, obviously not prepared to fully turn over the reins to her. He released a heavy breath, then relented. "Okay. I'll sit in the hallway."

"Away from the room," Layla added.

"Away from the room, but only if you call me so I can listen to the conversation."

Layla twisted her lips and thought for a second. Mason's proposal was a good compromise. She would talk to Anthony Lackey, and Mason would stay out of jail—at least for tonight.

"Okay. Deal."

Layla started the car and resumed her route to Memorial Hermann hospital. In less than ten minutes, she'd parked in the garage, cut the engine, and turned to Mason. "Ready?"

"Yes."

She moved to open the door, but Mason's firm grip on her wrist halted her movement. "Thank you, Layla."

"For what?"

"For having a clear head. For looking out for me and the good of the story. For being what I need right now."

"You're welcome."

Within milliseconds, Mason's strong palm was behind her head, drawing her into his personal space. His lips connected with hers, and she thought she'd lose her mind. She'd kissed many frogs, but right now, her lips circled against the proverbial prince's lips. Up until this moment in her life, all kisses were the same. But kissing Mason…her mind, her heart, her entire being were in sync while simultaneously off kilter. Thank goodness she was in the hospital's parking garage because she might need a doctor.

Her heart raced so quickly she thought it might jump out of her chest to find a doctor itself. Yet, an overwhelming sensation of peace and oneness washed over her. A feeling she couldn't explain. And for her, unexplained feelings meant danger. Layla broke the kiss but didn't back away. She opened her eyes to look at Mason. Did he experience the same thing—the same feeling of needing to stop, but also not wanting to? Needing more, but knowing more was dangerous?

She could never kiss him again.

Although kissing him was the best lip-lock experience she'd had in her life, it was too much. Their connection was too much. She'd known since she'd met him that they were connected.

Such a bond was too much.

∞

What had Mason done?

If Layla filed a sexual harassment claim against him back in the office, he wouldn't blame her, though he doubted it would come to that based on the fact she'd kissed him back. And the look in her eyes when they came up for air was seared in his mind. He'd kissed more than his fair share of women, but what he'd just experienced with Layla exceeded ordinary. Something else happened, though he couldn't be certain of what that was because he'd never experienced it before. And he couldn't find out because kissing her couldn't happen again. They were coworkers, and he needed to keep a clear head.

But his curiosity taunted him.

Would he have the same experience if he kissed her again? The turmoil of his inner man begged him to find out.

Layla's voice through his Bluetooth earbuds cut through his thoughts. They didn't say anything about the kiss after it happened. She and Mason just strolled into the hospital like nothing happened between them. And he could partially appreciate that. Though he wrote thousands of words regularly, he couldn't come up with the vernacular to describe what occurred between them.

Mason increased the volume on his earbuds and listened intently.

Layla's interview with Anthony Lackey was the only thing that kept his mind off kissing her again.

"Hi, Mr. Lackey. I'm Layla Langston, and I'm a journalist for *The Houston Exposure.* I'd like to talk to you regarding the news of your DNA at a recent crime scene."

Mason heard Anthony's voice, but couldn't understand what he said.

"What I'd like to know is why your DNA was found at the crime scene if you weren't there." A bout of silence passed before she added, "It's just you and me here, so you can tell me the truth. If you were declared innocent, why do the police have you in cuffs locked to your hospital bed?"

Mason waited for what seemed like an eternity for the man to respond.

When his voice sounded through Mason's earbuds, Mason leaned forward and closed his eyes, careful not to miss a single word.

His voice was hoarse, but Mason could understand him. "I didn't go to the rally. My guardian angel wanted me to go, but I didn't. Said he'd do it himself. Talk to my mom or my brother…the club downtown is where I was…the chief knows…my mom knows. I wasn't there. I didn't do it." Anthony Lackey coughed several times. "I don't mind owning up to my sins, but this ain't one of 'em. I shouldn't be in these."

Mason stiffened. And not because of the clinking of the man's handcuffs against the bed railing. Anthony mentioned a political rally—an event that had nothing to do with the night in question. Was he referencing his father's event? Was he confusing two different crimes because of the medication?

Layla asked, "Why are you in these cuffs if you weren't there?"

"You gotta tell the truth. I didn't do it." His words slurred.

Layla's calm voice must have helped matters because he answered all of her questions.

"Okay, that's why I'm here. For the truth. You mentioned the political rally. Can you tell me more about that?"

"My mom...my guardian angel...the police chief... You need to talk to..." His voice trailed off.

Layla called Anthony Lackey's name over and over. If Mason had to guess, the man had fallen asleep because of the medication. But he'd given them some information of value by confirming the chief and congresswoman were working together to bury something—Mason needed to find out what. And who was this guardian angel he mentioned?

Minutes later, Layla found him in the hallway.

Mason stood and stuffed his hands in his pockets. He didn't know what else to do with them other than wrap them around her, and that was inappropriate. He'd already tiptoed over professional boundaries. He didn't need to do so again in the same day that he'd kissed her.

"Did you hear that?" she asked while they retraced their steps toward the parking garage exit.

Mason nodded. He should really be focused on this story, but he couldn't help but wonder if the kiss affected her the same way it affected him. He assessed her as much as he could while navigating toward the exit. Layla didn't appear disturbed. She wore the same neutral expression as she always did, and that bothered him. But he couldn't address her lack of acknowledgment of what happened between them without addressing his lack of professionalism, so he didn't mention the kiss. Not mentioning it was for the best.

Mason cleared his throat. "Yes, I heard him. Sounds like the drugs he's on confirmed that his mother—the congresswoman—and the chief of police are in cahoots. We need to find out what they're covering up."

Layla nodded, but she appeared to be in deep thought. Not once did she give eye contact to Mason. "What if the chief and Congresswoman Lackey have a secret? Like, what if it's something that only the two of them know, and he's in her pocket?" Layla continued to spar off ideas. "What if they're watching each other's backs because they're in this together—to incriminate one is to incriminate the other?"

"Yeah, but what kind of secret would they be protecting? A business? A child?" Mason counted off.

Layla sucked in a chest full of air, and Mason was sure of it because he could see her chest inflate. "Oh, my goodness. What if they're lovers and she asked the chief to do something illegal for her, and he did it?"

Mason allowed Layla's thoughts to sink in while they walked back to her car. If Anthony Lackey were a secret lovechild between the two of them, that would be a reason for the chief not to arrest him.

"Why do you think he mentioned the political rally to you? The murder didn't take place at a rally."

"Could be because he attends them with his mother."

"Maybe, but what if he was talking about something else?" All Mason could think about was his father and how part of him believed there was foul play in the cause of the explosion that killed him. Layla likely wouldn't have the same line of thought.

She hesitated and he couldn't help but wonder if they shared the same thoughts, only she'd been afraid to mention it. "Then we should keep our eyes open. Let's not forget he mentioned his guardian angel. Twice. I'm interested in figuring out who that is and if they're important here. Think the guardian angel could be the chief?"

"It would make sense if we consider him and the congresswoman working together to cover something up."

When Mason and Layla arrived at Layla's car and the driver and passenger's side windows were smashed, he knew they were closer to the truth.

And someone was doing their best to make them step away.

CHAPTER THIRTEEN

Two weeks had passed since the kiss, the vandalism on both of their cars, and the realization that they hadn't gotten any closer to the truth. Layla knew these investigations took time, only she hoped they would be closer to solving the case and writing their story at this point. She'd already finished her first local story about the funding Lamar Consolidated School District needed for technological improvements and to build more schools.

Sure, Layla and Mason had their theories, but no solid proof. To date, he hadn't mentioned the kiss, and neither had she. If anything, Layla did her best not to put herself in a position to be kissed by him again. And it wasn't because she didn't enjoy those seconds they were physically and intimately close. Staying away from him was for the best because she enjoyed that kiss way too much.

She hadn't forgotten how his lips felt nor how her heart responded. In fact, her pulsing heart betrayed her whenever he was near, but thankfully he didn't know that. Layla believed in pursuing those things that made her feel good, but she had her limits. If anything felt too good, then it probably was. What she refused to let happen was to get swept up in some kind of romantic fantasy. She'd

117

convinced herself that the reason she liked the kiss so much was because she'd been out of the dating game for too long.

But that wasn't true. When she left her family's company, she also broke up with her boyfriend of six months. Jackson was a good guy, just not the one for her. No reason to allow a relationship that had expired to sit on the shelf.

Layla parked at a surface lot near Houston's Criminal Justice complex and waited for Mason to arrive. She hoped parking in an open lot would prevent her windows from being smashed. She had them repaired the next day after her car was vandalized a couple of weeks ago.

Like every other trip they'd made, they could have carpooled, but Layla ensured their meeting with her brother-in-law, District Attorney Marcel Singleton, was first thing that morning. That way, it would make sense if the two of them took separate cars because the meeting time would be at the start of their workday.

When she saw Mason's truck enter the parking lot, she cut her engine, climbed out of her car and met him in the middle of the lot. He was dressed in a long-sleeved white buttoned-down shirt that made her believe his biceps wanted freedom, and a matching navy necktie and pants. Of course, the tie was simply because they had a meeting with the DA because she hadn't seen him in one since they'd met.

She looked up and smiled at him. "Good morning. Ready to make some progress?"

"Morning. You have no idea." He held his stainless-steel coffee mug in one hand and took a sip. "You look nice today, by the way."

Layla glanced down at her casual indigo pantsuit and flats. "Thank you." She turned toward the building. "Let's get this show on the road. Marcel is expecting us."

"I appreciate you setting up this meeting. I know the DA doesn't get involved in situations where there haven't been any convictions, but hopefully this time will prove to be productive."

"Yeah, because we could use some movement."

Three days ago, Layla and Mason received word that HPD didn't tie Detective Mansfield's death to any active investigations. An unfortunate, random break-in that resulted in her death. Neither Layla nor Mason believed the story HPD gave the public, but at this juncture, they had nothing but their gut to lead them—no solid proof that would prove anything to the contrary.

Mason held out his hand to aid Layla in climbing the steps into the building. When they walked through the glass doors, she spotted Marcel. He strolled over to greet her with a hug.

After a tight squeeze, he pulled away. "Hey, sis. How are you and this new job?" He looked over her shoulder and shot Mason a confused expression.

"I take it Crystal hasn't told you much about it."

"Well, she said you'd taken a new position at *The Houston Exposure,* but it never occurred to me that you were working with Mason."

Marcel and Mason shook hands.

119

"Follow me to my office."

They trailed Marcel through the building. Compared to other government facilities she'd been in, this one seemed more up to date—or at least the shiny tile floors and lemon scent made her think the building was more modern.

Inside Marcel's office, he closed his door, gestured toward the two visitor's seats, rounded his cherry wood desk, and sat. He clasped his hands on the wooden surface and addressed Mason first.

"I'm sorry about what happened to your father, Mason. He was a good man."

"Thanks."

Layla perched on the edge of her seat. "We believe the police chief is working with Congresswoman Lackey to bury information about her son's involvement in a murder. Anthony Lackey's DNA was found at a murder scene, yet the police aren't doing anything about it."

Marcel leaned back in his seat and smoothed his hand along his crimson necktie. He held her gaze. "That's a serious accusation, Layla."

Mason inserted himself into the conversation. "The police haven't done their job, so it seems we have to do it for them. Are you familiar with the recent DNA evidence that puts Congresswoman Lackey's son at the murder scene of Flex Technology's COO?"

Marcel nodded. "Yes, but it also my understanding that the police determined his DNA was tainted in some way, and they weren't able to prove his involvement. Plus, he had an alibi."

Mason pressed. "And what do you know about Detective Mansfield's murder?"

Marcel folded his hands in his lap. "The police didn't find any evidence at the crime scene. So far, there are no suspects."

Mason scooted to the edge of his seat. "Don't you see the connection here? I mean, we know it's common for the police to have cold cases around, but c'mon. Don't you think it's a little odd that the detective investigating Anthony Lackey ends up dead? And not only does she end up murdered, but we're also getting the same story—no evidence, no suspects. And the commonality? Anthony Lackey. And we know Congresswoman Lackey has something to do with all of this as well."

Mason removed a document from his briefcase and slid it across the desk to Marcel. "And that piece of paper there tells us that the DNA under Detective Mansfield's fingernails belongs to the same person who murdered the COO of Flex Technology."

Marcel rubbed his chin and examined the paper. "Wow."

Layla jumped back in. "Right. So that's why we're coming to you. Is your office planning to do anything about this? Is this case even on your radar?"

"It hasn't been, and that's mostly because the police haven't charged anyone with either of their murders. You know how this goes. Mason knows the drill."

"Yeah, but as your sister-in-law, I'm asking you to do something about it. It's obvious there's some foul play going on here."

Marcel continued to read through the documents Mason had handed him. "I have to admit that it does sound suspicious."

Mason huffed. "Right. And if I remember correctly, one of your campaign promises was to make sure the right people were charged with their crimes. Right now, nothing is being done, Mr. DA."

Marcel jerked his head toward Mason. "There's a fine line. Don't cross it. You're a journalist and not a detective. I'd hate to see my office prosecuting you. Let the authorities handle it."

Mason leaned back in his seat and folded his arms across his chest. "That's all I'm asking for...justice to be served."

Layla shared the information she and Mason had gathered up until now, and Marcel agreed with them. There wasn't enough evidence to charge Anthony Lackey, especially considering he had an alibi. And so did his brother, who would be the next likely suspect. They needed the missing link—something to tie this investigation together—though Marcel advised against them doing detective work.

"I'll ask questions of my friends at the precinct to put a little fire under them. We'll get some answers. Maybe a new detective can find something Detective Mansfield may have missed."

Mason stretched his arm across the desk and shook Marcel's hand. "Thank you. I owe you, man."

"Just look out for my sister here, and we'll be even."

"That goes without question."

Layla stood. "Thanks for anything you can do to help us."

Marcel stood and rounded the table. "No problem. I have to look out for family."

Marcel and Mason shook hands again.

Before Layla trailed Mason out of Marcel's office, he called, "Mason, let me talk with Layla for a second before you all leave. Family matter."

Mason closed the door behind him.

Marcel lowered his voice, folded his arms in a big brother stance, and cocked his head to the side. "Do you know what you're getting yourself into?"

"I appreciate your concern, Marcel, but yes, I do. I'm fine. This is my job."

"You should be writing stories about teacher pay raises or better healthcare for senior citizens. You're a journalist, not a detective."

"You're right. I am a journalist, and this is not the only story I'm working on. But, in this case, the only way to write the story is to dig a little harder than the police did. And if that means playing detective, then that's what we have to do."

"Do your parents and sisters know what you're running around town doing?"

Layla gripped his shoulders. "I'm fine, trust me. I won't do anything that will get me hurt."

Marcel looked toward heaven and shook his head. "While I believe you, we can't control other folks' actions, especially folks you think are covering up a murder, which is why I'm going to make sure there's a detective looking into the case involving Congresswoman Lackey's son. This is real, Layla."

She knew the realness of the situation way more than she was willing to share. Layla hadn't told anyone about the damage to her and Mason's vehicles—a scare tactic to get her and Mason to end their investigation.

"I know, and I promise to be careful. Plus, I trust Mason. He'd convince our boss to remove me from his story if he thought my life was in danger."

"And what is the deal between you two, anyway?"

Layla gave him a quick hug. "Nothing at all. That's my cue to leave, though. See you soon."

∞

Mason escorted Layla back to her car. And for once, he was glad she didn't ride with him because he had something he needed to do alone. The fight within couldn't leave this investigation in the hands of the police again, no matter what promises the district attorney made. He was only one man and not all powerful. Mason didn't get the feeling that one phone call from the DA would get him the answers he needed.

No.

Ultimately, getting the answers for this story rested upon Mason's shoulders.

Layla turned to face him when they made it to her car. "Does the meeting with Marcel make you feel any better?"

"Not as much as I thought it would, but I appreciate him doing what he can to get the investigation moving again, though I can't promise I'll step aside and wait for the cops to do nothing."

The light in her eyes twinkled as she gave the kind of smile that made him believe she had similar thoughts. "I didn't think you would. You don't strike me as the kind of man who'd leave his fate up to someone else."

"When I was a kid, my mom would often say if you wanted something done right, you have to do it yourself. I believe this is one of those scenarios."

"Good thing you've got me to help in this do-it-yourself situation."

"You mean to tell me your brother-in-law didn't tell you to stay in your lane. Leave me to my own demise."

Layla tossed her head back and chuckled. Her silky hair danced behind her shoulders in the breeze. "He wouldn't be himself if he didn't offer his opinion about my safety, but as I told him, I'm simply doing my job. I know my limitations."

Mason cocked his head to the side. "Is that so? Your limitations as it relates to what?"

"Everything. This job. You." She clamped her lips shut.

Mason should let the Freudian slip slide, but he couldn't bypass the opportunity to probe a little further. Until now, neither of them had made any references to their shared kiss or emotional connection.

He stepped closer. "Why would you need limitations when it comes to me, Layla?"

"I think you know the answer to your own question. For the same reason you have limitations when it comes to me."

"Where'd you get that idea? I've never said that."

"You didn't have to. Your actions after we kissed said it for you."

She had no idea how much restraint he needed to keep from kissing her every day. Even now. But they didn't need any distractions at work. Mason took a step back because if he stayed as close as he was to her, he'd pull her into his arms to see if they'd have the same experience as the last time they kissed.

Mason cleared his throat. "What actions? Be specific."

"You've been acting like the kiss never happened. Like it was a mistake."

The uncertainty in her eyes bothered him. But he couldn't blame her hesitation because she didn't know how thoughts of her kept him up at night, how he thought of her first thing every morning, or how he had to intentionally keep a safe distance from her while at work.

"Well, let's clear the air right now. First, kisses aren't mistakes. I don't understand how anyone could accidentally kiss another person. I kissed you because I wanted to—because for a moment, I gave my emotions control. I should have been stronger than that. Whatever I feel for you cannot be a distraction in this assignment. So, if you want to call that a limitation, then I guess I do have them when it comes to you."

A satisfied smile spread across her full lips. "Well, okay then. Thanks for clearing that up." She turned to open her car door, but he maneuvered around her to open it. "I guess I'll see you in the office."

"I have a quick errand to run, but I'll be in the office as soon as I'm done."

When Layla climbed inside, he closed the door and stood there with his hands stuffed in his pockets.

"Mason."

He lifted his chin when Layla called out to him.

"I guess we have the same limitation."

CHAPTER FOURTEEN

Mason navigated his truck into Memorial Hermann's parking garage. Though he allowed Layla to handle the first interview with Anthony Lackey, he wanted—well, needed—to look into the man's eyes and see if he was telling the truth or if his interview with Layla was an act. Either way, Mason had already convinced himself of Lackey's involvement because he didn't believe the man would confess his guilt anyway.

When Mason stepped off the elevator and rounded the final corner down the hall where Lackey's room was, he spotted two men dressed in black on either side of his door. As he got closer, he identified the listening devices in their ears. That could only mean Congresswoman Melissa Lackey was inside.

And to think he'd planned to pay her a visit eventually. Today must be his lucky day—that is, if the security guards wouldn't prevent him from getting inside. When Mason approached, he saw one of them speaking into the headpiece.

Mason nodded. "Good morning, gentlemen."

"Morning. You can't go in there," the guard who recently spoke into his headpiece said. He moved to stand in front of the door, blocking Mason's entry. The man stood the same height as Mason, while his partner was at least four inches taller.

He needed answers, so the last thing he wanted to do was cause problems or even appear to cause problems, especially in a hospital.

"Is there a timeframe on that? I need to talk to Anthony."

The guard folded his arms across his chest and cocked his head to the side as if to say, "What do you think?" Still, Mason didn't budge. And he wasn't the least bit intimidated by the guy. He had to maintain his composure and patience because this trip wouldn't be in vain.

Seconds later, the door creaked open, and Congresswoman Lackey poked her head around the bodyguard's shoulder. "Mason. Walter Sterling's son. I recognize him from photos with his late father. He's good to come inside, Devin."

Devin stepped aside to allow Mason entry.

Dressed like she was prepared to spend a day on Capitol Hill, the woman wore a black skirt suit, heels, and a full face of makeup. She even wore the bun on top of her head that he'd become accustomed to seeing on TV. Even with her heels on, she still stood about six inches shorter than him.

The congresswoman wrapped her arms around Mason's shoulder with a familiarity and closeness they didn't share. In fact, he'd never had any contact with her before this point. "I'm sorry about what happened to your father. He is definitely missed." She backed away and patted his arm. "How are you? And what can we do for you?"

"I'm alright. First, I know this is bad timing considering Anthony is lying in a hospital bed—"

She interrupted him. "Yet, that didn't stop you from coming."

"Him being here is what led me here. I'm sure you've heard of the DNA that links Anthony to the murder scene of the COO of Flex Technology. I want to talk with him."

She dismissed him with a wave of her hand. "He was cleared of any wrongdoing. Anthony wasn't even in the area the evening of the crime."

"Was he with you?"

She led him over to the sitting area where there was a small sofa and two chairs. "Why don't you have a seat?"

Mason sat, but didn't speak.

She cast worried eyes in the direction of her son who lay in the bed asleep. Pale skin. Thin frame. Not guilty, yet still handcuffed to the bed. "About five years ago, my son had a blood transfusion, which is the only explanation for the blood match. I know you want answers, but they aren't in this room."

"Why is he still handcuffed to the bed if he isn't guilty?"

"We're working with the hospital to release the medical information to the police without violating their privacy policies."

As much as he didn't want to, Mason bought her story. Sounded legitimate. And as of this moment, he didn't have any proof as to the contrary. Still, something didn't feel right. Memories of Layla's interview with Anthony came to mind. The guardian angel. Mentioning the political rally that had nothing to do with the murder of Flex Technology's COO.

"Who is Anthony's guardian angel?"

Her eyebrows shot up, but she quickly lowered them to keep a straight face. That wasn't a question she expected, Mason was certain. "I don't know what you mean."

It wouldn't be wise of him to share that Layla already questioned Anthony. The congresswoman would probably have him thrown out, so he changed his question. "I'm talking about the blood transfusion Anthony received. Who donated the blood?"

"Oh, we don't know. We're just thankful the transfusion saved his life."

That part of her story he didn't believe. She'd been twisting the ring on her left finger since he mentioned the guardian angel. Maybe Anthony's medication hadn't influenced his responses to Layla.

She rubbed her hands along her skirt. "Well, if that's all, I'd like to get back to my son now. There's no need to wake him for this. And for what it's worth," she reached out and squeezed his hand, "Again, I'm sorry about your father."

"Thank you, Congresswoman."

He had to ask. Needed to know if the political rally Anthony spoke of was his father's event. A long shot? Yes. But the woman hadn't told him the truth about this guardian angel business. What else was this family hiding?

"Do you believe the explosion that killed him was an accident?"

Her forehead and the skin around her eyes creased. "Why would it be anything but? Wasn't that what the investigation revealed?"

"Yea, but we can never be too sure these days. Politics can be dirty," he said, hoping to get a rise out of her.

"You're right. And filled with dirty rumors. It's a nasty business sometimes."

"Indeed, but behind every dirty rumor or speculative story, somewhere lies the truth."

She cut her eyes at him. If he didn't know better, he'd think she was pretending to be kind to him. Or maybe not kind, but tolerating him enough to tell him what she thought he wanted to hear so that he'd leave her family alone. And at this point, Mason was almost okay with that scenario, especially if what she said about Anthony's blood transfusion was fact. In that case, he didn't have much information to go on unless he missed something in Detective Mansfield's notes.

"I don't know anything about the explosion, but I did hear that underhanded business was going on in your father's political camp. Word is that he had plans to release documents concerning details about political bribes and embezzlement of taxpayer funds." She spoke as if she'd never do such a thing, but Mason didn't care about her politics at the moment.

"Are you insinuating the explosion was not an accident?"

Her expression remained emotionless. Mason found it difficult to read her. "The investigation revealed it was an accident, so I'm not insinuating anything."

"Since my father was challenging you for your seat, was it you he wanted to expose?"

She leaped to her feet and jammed her finger in his direction. "Of course not. And if you recall, I wasn't the only one running against him." She counted on her fingers. "There's also the governor, the CEO of Modular Industries, and the CEO of Better Breads & Buns. Maybe you should talk to them."

"How do you know I haven't already spoken to them?"

She walked to the door. "This conversation isn't going anywhere. I think it's best you leave."

Mason stood and followed her to the door. She opened it and stood to the side to allow him room to exit.

"And while I hope you find the answers you seek about that COO's murder, please don't come around my family again. We have our own issues to contend with."

He nodded and strolled back toward the elevator. Time was what he needed but didn't have enough of. Time to process his conversation with her. Time to piece together everything she didn't say. Anthony may not be guilty of murder, but the congresswoman was guilty of something—and he vowed to find out the truth.

∞

"Mason, Mason," Layla called out to him, but he didn't turn around to respond. It had been the third time she'd all but yelled his name.

But since he wouldn't answer her, she followed him to see what had his attention so occupied that he couldn't hear her voice, or at least chose to ignore it. Layla hadn't been concerned about trailing him quietly. It wasn't as if he heard her or acknowledged her presence in the first place.

He walked at a steady pace with his eyes focused on his phone, which was weird. She'd always known him to be aware of his surroundings. And considering it was dark outside, Layla would think he'd be more cautious. Crazy incidents happened on the streets of Houston all the time, especially to those who weren't paying attention. But nothing about his focused demeanor made her believe he had any concerns.

With each passing step, she sensed a heaviness in the atmosphere.

"Mason where are you going?" she asked. The unsteadiness of her own voice made her nervous.

He picked up his pace, and so did Layla. However, no matter how fast she walked, she couldn't seem to catch up to him.

When Mason rounded the corner, he stopped in front of an abandoned brick mom-and-pop convenience store where he came face-to-face with a man who was about his same height and build wearing all black. He looked over Mason's shoulder. "You came alone as agreed. Good. Then this should be easy."

Alone? I'm right here. *"Mason, what are you doing? Who is this? Why didn't you invite me to this meeting? We're a team."*

Ignoring her, Mason said, "Yeah. Now give me the information you promised."

It was dark, but Layla saw the evil gleam in the man's eyes, illuminated by the streetlights, even though she couldn't make out his features. In fact, she couldn't make out much of anything. It was as if the three of them were the only ones in the area. No cars. No people. No other lights. She got alley vibes, though the space was more open.

The man reached inside of his jacket. "Oh, you'll never have any more questions after this."

A loud shot rang out, followed by another, accompanied by a flare. Mason collapsed. Blood poured from his chest.

Layla's breath constricted like she was the one who'd been shot. Paralyzed with fear, she stood there on shaky limbs, knowing she'd be next now that the man could see her face. But the shot never came. The man laughed an eerily, haunting laugh and walked away as if his job was done.

Still reeling from the shock, Layla dropped to her knees by Mason's side. She pressed two fingers to the side of his neck, praying for a pulse. "C'mon, Mason. You've got to pull through this." Her tears dripped on his lifeless face as she leaned close to his ear. "Please don't die. I need you."

Layla jerked to a sitting position in bed. Her face and neck were soaked with tears. She wiped her eyes with the backs of her hands. That dream felt real. Too real. And based on her feelings revealing themselves through that dream, a real she couldn't handle. Sure, she didn't want anything to happen to Mason. They'd become good friends in the past month. But even more, she had feelings for him.

Layla scrambled out of bed to clean herself up for work. The steam from the shower reminded her of the fog in her dream, which wasn't evident until she and Mason rounded the corner and stopped in front of the convenience store. The whole scene was like something she'd seen play out in a couple of movies. It would always be dark and foggy with the suspenseful music that made her heart race.

She couldn't shake the images from her mind. What bothered her most was she didn't believe Mason would put himself in a position to get hurt. Or meet anyone in a dark alley. Was he blinded by his desire for justice? Or was she the one who didn't understand what lengths he'd go through to get his story?

Layla went through her routine on autopilot, stifled with the feeling that something was wrong. What if the dream was a warning that Mason's life was now in danger? Or could it be her mind playing tricks on her, revealing her feelings about his hospital visit and encounter with the congresswoman?

Her cell phone chimes cut through her thoughts. Marcel's name and number lit the screen. Had he found out something already?

"Hey, Marcel. What's up?" She held her breath.

"Crys is in labor. We're on our way to The Woman's Hospital."

Layla squealed. Crystal wasn't due for another three weeks, so baby news wasn't what she expected to hear. "Okay. Have you called anyone else yet?"

"No, you're the first."

"I'll let everyone know and meet you there."

After she hung up with Marcel, she called Ava, who was in Atlanta's airport with Zack. Their flight had just been delayed, so she promised to come to the hospital as soon as she made it back to Houston. Their parents were in New York celebrating a friend's fiftieth wedding anniversary, but were now cutting their trip short.

Layla finished getting dressed with more energy. A new baby would take her mind off her intrusive, illusive dreams, or so she hoped. Layla couldn't help the nagging in her mind that seemed to indicate Mason was on the wrong path, and she had to do something to keep the dream—well, nightmare—from happening.

She couldn't lose him.

CHAPTER FIFTEEN

L ayla had spent the last six hours in the hospital with Crystal and Marcel, awaiting the arrival of her first nephew. The only time she and Marcel left Crystal's side was when the doctor instructed them so that Crystal could receive her epidural. From that point on, Crystal didn't complain of any pain from her contractions.

After the doctor assured Marcel that Crystal hadn't fully dilated and his son wouldn't be arriving anytime soon, he went to the hospital's cafeteria for food.

As if Crystal had been waiting for an opportunity for them to be alone, she grilled Layla about her new job as soon as the door closed behind Marcel. "Before we get into what's going on with you and this Mason you're working with, convince me that I shouldn't be worried about what you're doing over at *The Houston Exposure*."

Layla scooted a chair to her sister's bedside. "I'm sure Marcel exaggerated whatever he told you. Mason is mentoring me while I help him with a story he's working on concerning one of our local congresswomen."

"I hear you, but you are not a detective, so don't be running around town acting like one and getting yourself in trouble."

She wouldn't expect anything less from her oldest sister, but what Marcel and Crystal seemed to have forgotten was that she was a grown woman who could make her own decisions. Layla rolled her eyes toward heaven.

"Sis, you don't have to worry about me, especially not now. I'm good. All I want you to be concerned with is delivering this baby." Layla rubbed Crystal's protruding belly.

"Honey, I feel like a stuffed turkey."

Layla laughed along with Crystal. "But, you're still beautiful and strong." Layla clasped one of Crystal's swollen hands in her own. "I appreciate you and Marcel looking out for me, but I'm fine. Promise."

Crystal adjusted herself in the bed so that she sat more upright. She eyed Layla for a moment as if deciding whether she wanted to believe her. "Well, what's this Marcel tells me about the chemistry between you and Mason? Tell me about this guy."

Layla chuckled. "I'm pretty sure *chemistry* is not the word Marcel used. Sounds like something you came up with all on your own."

"He didn't have to. I know how to read between the lines, but if you want to know what his words were, he said something to the effect of both of you giving each other the eye when you thought he wasn't looking. My honey also mentioned he saw you two in the parking lot looking like you were about to lock lips."

Layla laughed a little harder, hoping to mask her embarrassment. She remembered the moment all too well because a part of her had hoped Mason would do just that. She secretly wanted to kiss him again to verify if what she felt the first time was real. In fact, she'd dreamed about that moment—a more pleasant dream than some of the others she'd had as of late. Who else saw them?

"Nothing happened."

Crystal laughed. "You look like Momma just caught you sneaking extra snacks."

Layla giggled because of the memories Crystal's comment brought about. She'd been caught far too many times with extra snacks in her backpack and under her bed pillow.

"You may as well give up the goods. You may not have kissed him in the parking lot, but you have kissed him, haven't you?"

Layla avoided eye contact with Crystal and made a show of adjusting Crystal's gown.

Crystal clapped. "I knew it the moment Marcel told me because you don't allow anyone into your personal space like that. So, give me the juice. What's going on with you two?"

Layla inhaled deeply and exhaled with a sigh. "Nothing, actually. I think we were both caught up in the moment, you know? We've been working well together. And with me assisting him, he'd taken it to heart for a second. But we're good. We've put it behind us." Layla worked to convince herself and Crystal.

Crystal threw her head back against the pillow. "Ah, here we go again. First, Ava, now you. So, work is the reason you guys aren't exploring your interest in each other?"

"Basically, yes. Any exploration would be a distraction."

Crystal waved her hand. "*Pssh.* Girl, those are excuses and lies y'all are telling yourselves. If there aren't any work policies against dating, then date the man if you want to. You and Mason could be missing out on something great with each other. Do you remember the advice I gave Ava a couple of years ago?"

"I don't, but I'm sure you're about to remind me."

Crystal chuckled. "And you'd be right." She took both of Layla's hands into her own and gazed into her eyes like she was about to say something profound. "Nothing can stop two grown people who want to be together. Besides, you know the saying, 'the heart wants what the heart wants.' Don't deny the heart because you don't know how long either of you have on this earth. 'Time waits for no one.'"

"You've got all the clichés today, huh?"

Crystal shrugged. "I'm just saying."

"I hear you, but this is not like Ava's situation."

The door creaked open. Crystal and Layla turned to see who walked in.

Ava shuffled to the bed with her arms wide. She hugged Layla first, then Crystal. "Did I just hear my name?"

Crystal answered, "You sure did. Layla has a thing for her coworker, Mason, and she's afraid to date him because they work together. Said something about dating him would be a distraction. Sound familiar?"

Ava sat on the opposite side of the bed with her eyes and mouth wide. "Seriously. Give me all the details."

Layla didn't comment on what Crystal said, but instead asked, "Where's Zack?"

"Went to see his brothers. He'll come by later. Why are you changing the subject? That's okay." Ava whipped out her phone to search for Mason on *The Houston Exposure*'s website while Crystal filled her in on Layla's dilemma. Well, it wasn't a dilemma if you asked Layla. She and Mason had already decided how they'd handle the situation.

"*Hmmm.* So do you have any feelings for him?"

Layla shrugged. "I'm not sure," she lied.

Ava audibly sucked in a breath. Her eyes widened, and her lips formed into an "O." "Look at your face. You do."

Layla pursed her lips to one side. "You've been married five seconds, and now you're an expert."

Ava chuckled. "Not an expert. I just know what you're dealing with. I'm not worried though, Crys. Maybe she's waiting on one of those dreams to tell her what to do. Either way, if her face is any indication, she won't pass on the opportunity to see what Mason is all about." She turned her phone toward Crystal and Layla and wriggled her eyebrows. "He's handsome, too."

"You know I looked him up the moment Marcel told me about him."

The sisters shared a laugh until the fun in Crystal's eyes turned into a panic-stricken expression. "I can't feel a thing, but look at the spikes on that machine. Get the nurse and call Marcel. I think it might be time."

∞

With Layla's sister going into labor yesterday, Mason didn't get a chance to see Layla at all. The office and work were different without her presence. He'd go as far as to say empty. He navigated his truck to his father's house, parked in the driveway, and cut the engine. Mason couldn't bring himself to go inside, so he waited for Layla to arrive. A week ago, she'd offered to help him pack up some of his father's things. He had to prepare the house for sale at some point. He'd put off the task long enough.

According to the time on his dashboard, she should be there in less than ten minutes based on the estimated time of arrival she'd given him when they talked on the phone twenty minutes ago.

Mason sat in the driver's seat, restrained by dread and his seatbelt. The grass and flowerbed were neat, thanks to the landscapers Mason paid to keep the yard tidy. The one-story brick home he'd grown up in was nestled in a secluded neighborhood north of Houston in The Woodlands. It looked perfect on the outside, but only Mason could decipher the truth. There was nothing left in that old house but memories. Memories he wasn't ready to relive. No life. No family. Only his past.

He swallowed the rock in his throat when he looked in the rearview mirror and saw Layla park her car behind his. She climbed out of her two-door coupe looking even more beautiful than the last time he saw her, which was only a few days ago. But still, today she looked like the rainbow after a violent storm. And of course, she wore the smile that made his heart do crazy things because good things were happening in her life, especially with the birth of her first nephew.

Mason climbed out of his truck to meet her. When they were a few feet apart, he stuffed his hands in his pockets. "Hey. How's the baby?"

Layla beamed and pulled out her phone to show him photos. The showing of all her teeth warmed his sad heart. "He is so precious and so tiny. He put my sister through a lot of pain to get here, but I'm sure she'd say it was all worth it. Everyone is excited, and I'm sure it goes without saying that the poor guy will be spoiled."

Mason chuckled. "That's good to hear. And how are you?"

"Tired, but good. I'm more concerned about you though, Mr-visiting-the-congresswoman-without-your-mentee."

"I told you about the visit so don't hold it against me."

"You haven't been investigating anything else without me, have you?"

"I wouldn't dream of it."

Layla threw her head back and chuckled.

"Speaking of dreams, have you had any more, especially about work?" He tilted his head to one side and paid attention to her eyes. They were always a telltale sign of whether she delivered the entire truth. She was a terrible liar.

Layla looked him in the eyes, almost as if she were willing herself to hold her gaze steady. "No, not really. Well, nothing important."

He didn't buy her answer any more than he'd buy a pair of five-hundred-dollar shoes, but he couldn't get into the details of her dreams or what they might mean right now. This was the time to face reality—a reality he hadn't been able to fully accept. For him, not coming to this house and preparing it for sale was license to hold on to the falsity that his father wasn't really gone. That he wasn't now alone in this world. No parents. No siblings. Just him.

Mason released a heavy stream of air. "I've put this off long enough. Thanks for coming over to help."

Layla studied him for seconds too long—seconds that made him feel vulnerable and uncomfortable. She took one of his hands in hers. "Are you ready? It's okay if you need to spend a little more time out here before you go in."

Mason massaged away the tightness swelling in his throat. "No, I'm fine. It's time."

Layla searched his eyes, as if looking for a reason not to believe him. Finally, she nodded. "Okay then. Let's go."

She never released his hand, and based on the emotions rolling inside of him, he didn't want her to.

He led her up the cemented walkway, squeezing her hand tighter than he should have considering the nature of their relationship. Rosebushes on either side spoke to a refreshing and renewal he didn't feel. When they made it to the front door, Mason hesitated before entering the code in the electronic keypad he'd talked his father into purchasing weeks before he died. He took another winded breath before typing in the passcode.

Clearing out his father's house had to be done.

When the keypad beeped, signaling the door was unlocked, Mason twisted the handle and pushed the door open. But he couldn't cross the threshold. The woodsy scent wafted to where he stood, beckoning him inside to face his reality.

Layla looked up at him and squeezed his hand in the most reassuring embrace he'd ever received. Though she hadn't lost a parent, she seemed to know how he felt and how to handle the delicate situation. And that, he could appreciate. "Everything will be okay. I'm with you, Mason."

He didn't answer, but he looked at her then shifted his attention back toward the empty corridor, where no one would greet him again.

Ever.

She waited for him to take the first step forward. When he was ready, which seemed like an eternity instead of minutes, he crossed the entrance, but couldn't bring himself to walk into the living room. Memories of him spending time with his mother and father from childhood to a few years ago flooded his mind. Why did this have to happen to him?

Mason cleared his throat and pushed through the pain.

Without letting go of the comfort and assurance of Layla's hand, he led her into his father's man cave—a safe place to start clearing things out. There, his father kept private documents and mailings to review later but never did. He knelt next to the leather ottoman and lifted the top. It overflowed with paper—some of which he'd think would be kept in a more secure place.

Layla knelt alongside him.

His name written in his father's handwriting on a yellow sticky note attached to a manila folder drew his attention.

Mason,

If you're reading this, then I'm probably dead or seriously injured, and it isn't by accident.

With caution, Mason removed the brown file folder on top of the pile and peeled it open. The first document looked almost like a rap sheet with Congresswoman Lackey's photo attached to it. A burning sensation coursed through his entire being. Had she looked him in the eye and lied to him when he spoke with her in the hospital? He'd already presumed she wasn't telling the complete truth, but to see that his father had dirt on her gave her ammunition and motive.

Before reading a single word, Mason surmised the document confirmed her involvement in his father's death.

The explosion wasn't an accident.

Only God in Heaven would keep her from Mason's vengeance.

CHAPTER SIXTEEN

Layla's heart broke for Mason. It was one thing to lose a parent, but an entirely different situation when one had to seek justice and answers for a parent's death. The selfish part of her wondered why she had to meet him now, when he was hurting and clearly emotionally unavailable. What was the purpose of meeting him? To help him figure out what happened to his father? Or, based on what her last dream insinuated, save Mason's life?

She wouldn't question God. At least not right now. Mason needed her. And maybe she needed him, too.

Layla couldn't ignore the warmth flowing through her being and the comfort she experienced when she was only trying to help him work through his grief. As much as she didn't want her thoughts to scurry down the rabbit hole of what-if, Crystal's advice hung in the back of her mind. They were grown, and they could get through this together. But how could Layla be certain that Mason wouldn't be falling for her for the wrong reasons? Reasons like the fact that she was here when he needed someone to depend on? To help him with his story and find out what happened to his father? To be the shoulder he could lean on? To be the person he could trust in this time of crisis?

She was overthinking the situation.

"I knew it."

Mason's comment cut through her wayward thoughts.

Layla rubbed his back to calm him and spoke in her most soothing voice. "Let's not jump to any conclusions before we consider all the facts."

He held up the paper in the file for her to read. She scooted closer to him and held one side of the folder. The proximity of closeness to him made her hands tremble a little, so she gripped the folder with an even tighter grasp to still her nerves.

"Wow. The money she received from these kickbacks is insane. How did your dad get this information?" She flipped the page to read more about Congresswoman Lackey's embezzlement and shifting of government contracts to businesses she favored and profited from in the last five years. And that was just the information Walter Sterling had in his file. She'd been in congress for the last fifteen years. Her dirty deeds probably dated just as far back, only there wasn't any proof in the current document Layla had her hands and eyes on.

Mason sat on the floor with his feet flat and forearms resting against his knees. He frowned and shook his head as if in deep thought. "But it still doesn't make sense. She mentioned this in our conversation. Congresswoman Lackey had to know I'd investigate."

Layla moved into a sitting position next to him. Memories of her most recent dream came to her forethought. Could the reason Congresswoman Lackey told Mason of the embezzlement be because she planned to have him killed so that the information would be buried with him? Shoot, was she the one who got rid of Detective Mansfield? Did Chief Gritlock know?

To keep her thoughts from spiraling, she pushed herself back to her knees and rested over the storage ottoman. "You're right, but that can't be the whole story. Let's keep digging."

She waited for Mason's okay before she removed anything because she didn't want him to feel like she was disrespecting his father's things, no matter the situation. When he nodded his agreement, she reached inside and pulled out the next file folder. She flipped it open and skimmed the contents of the first page.

"This is incriminating evidence against the assistant mayor who was in the congressional race against your dad." She handed the folder to Mason and reached inside the ottoman for the next one.

The next file had photos and documents of the governor involved in the same unethical situations. Bribery. Unequal distribution of government contracts. Misuse of funds received by donors. And even a long list of women willing to testify of sexual harassment—the *me too* movement. "Goodness. What is this man not guilty of?" She passed the file on to Mason.

"Who?" he asked while accepting the file.

She and Mason sat in silence. The sound of pages turning, folders flipping, and soft breathing was the music to their ears. Layla typically had an opinion about everything, but in a situation so delicate, she felt like she had to tiptoe around Mason's feelings. While he hadn't shown any signs of weakness, she couldn't help but wonder about the state of mind he must be in.

After he skimmed through the file, Mason peered inside the ottoman and sifted through the remaining documents. "There have to be at least ten additional folders in here. At this rate, any of these people could have had something to do with the explosion, or at least had motive."

Layla thought for a moment. "That's true, but we need to narrow the list down to people who knew he had this information."

Mason gave her one of those you-already-know-the-answer-to-that glances. "For starters, we know Congresswoman Lackey knew."

Layla sucked the air between her teeth. She was too obvious to blame. "Yeah, that's true, but it couldn't be her. Like you said, she mentioned this when you saw her at the hospital. If anything, she may have an idea about who else knows your father had this dirt on everyone. And another question to consider: Who gave the evidence to him and what did he intend to do with it?"

Mason rubbed his chin. "Congresswoman Lackey said he planned to use it to get the other politicians to drop out of the race, but I don't believe it. That's not my pops. He wouldn't do anything like that. If nothing else, he was a fair man."

Layla slid to the floor and sat in front of Mason with both feet crossed underneath her. She practiced her soothing voice again. "Okay, of the two of us, I'm the one who's impartial, so let's just consider for a moment that your dad would've used the information he had about everyone else in the race, or even if it were you. How would you go about letting your opponents know you knew their dirty little deeds?"

Mason didn't like the way this conversation was headed, based on the you-need-to-tread-carefully look in his eyes. But still, he answered. "I wouldn't leave a paper trail. Maybe I'd mention it while shaking their hand before or after a debate."

"Right. Sounds like something the average politician would do."

"And let's say that's what my dad did, but let me go on record and say I don't think he would've done so. He obviously made someone nervous."

"I don't think just someone, likely everyone, because they all would've had something to lose."

Mason nodded. "I can agree with that. Now with that in mind, who had the most to lose?"

"These are all high-powered folks—some already in the political arena like the assistant mayor and governor. The rest of these," she said, flipping through the files, "are all well-known businessmen in the local area, so that means their reputation and businesses would be in jeopardy if any of this information were to get out."

"You mean, when we expose everything and tell the whole truth. That's what *The Houston Exposure* is all about."

Layla admired Mason's dedication. But would he be willing to put a stain on his dad's memory if he were somehow mixed up in all of this? She couldn't bring herself to ask, especially when the question wasn't warranted.

"Right, so let's think about what we know. If we go along with thinking your father told these folks he had this information, he pissed them off, and they decided to do something about it."

"You're thinking the explosion that killed my father wasn't an accident?"

At this point, she didn't think she'd have to say the words, but maybe he needed her to confirm his thoughts. "Based on what we've read, and the sticky note from your father, it's highly unlikely the explosion was an accident. I believe it was planned."

He fixed his gaze on her with a frown covering his features. However, she sensed he wasn't looking at her, but thinking and whatever the thought had disturbed him. Mason picked up a few of the files and flipped them open to look at the headshots again. "I'm certain I saw at least three of these men in the crowd at my father's last fundraising event."

"Really? Who?"

Mason opened each folder to show her the photos.

Her breath caught. She and Mason made eye contact. The pain in his eyes was different than before. The facts were clear.

The files before them.

The conversation with Congresswoman Lackey.

The men at his father's political fundraiser.

The explosion.

The note from his father.

None of this information could be coincidence.

"I'm sorry, Mason."

His Adam's apple bobbed up and down, then he released a heavy breath. Instead of acknowledging her sympathy, he said, "We need to go through these files and cross reference them with Detective Mansfield's notes. Maybe she was looking into one of them as part of an ongoing investigation. Congresswoman Lackey is definitely a link between my father's death and her son's crimes. Let's see what we can piece together."

Finally, progress—but not the progress she envisioned.

A sense of dread hovered over her like a dark cloud threatening a storm. They were treading in deep water. She could feel the pressure mounting in her chest, creating a heaviness she couldn't shake.

"Well, sounds like we have a plan."

Today was the first time since starting this assignment that Layla felt like they were getting closer to finding answers. She just hoped those answers didn't lead them in such a way where she'd find her nightmares about Mason's death coming true. Her heart wasn't prepared to be without him.

∞

Mason left the room and returned with a box they could use to pack and transport the dossiers to his home. Layla had removed the files and stacked them in a neat pile on the floor next to where she sat. They were leveled up to her chest.

She reached for the box. "Of course, you'd go and find the perfect size, wouldn't you?"

"It just happened to be the first box I could find in the garage."

Mason chuckled and eased down to the floor next to her. His knee brushed hers. That little organ inside of his chest responded wildly, which was insane. He'd been in close proximity with this woman for the past couple of months. Being near her shouldn't affect him, yet he had no control over his emotions when it came to her.

He chalked his overcharged and unhinged emotions up to his grief. At least that was the lie he chose to believe. In truth, everything about Layla captivated him. Beyond her outward beauty, her intoxicating scent, which stayed with him hours after she'd left his presence, and the experience he had when he kissed her, their emotional bond tightened with every moment they spent together. She was smart, compassionate, lighthearted, and a pleasure to be around. When he wasn't with her, he may as well have been because she was all he thought about unless his mind was wrapped up in the development of this story. And even still, this investigation brought his thoughts back to her because she'd been with him every step since she started working at *The Houston Exposure*.

Layla put the files in the box then leaned over to double check the ottoman for anything she might have missed. She swept her hands at the base. "*Ooh,* looks like your dad had electronic records."

She dropped the thumb drive into Mason's palm.

"I didn't think he ever listened to me when I told him to use electronic storage instead of killing trees with paper. Well done, Pops." He shoved it into his back pocket.

155

Layla bit the side of her lip. Another thing she did when hesitating.

"You're holding back on me. I can see it in your face. What's on your mind?"

She folded the flaps on the box and rested her weight against it. "Do you think there may be anything else in here we need to find? Any other place where your father may have kept something that could help us find out what happened to him?"

Mason stood. He stretched his hand and helped Layla to her feet. "Let's take a look in his office."

He'd come to his father's house to make progress in preparing it for sale, but now he had a new mission.

Mason picked up the box and led her out of his father's man cave, down the hall to the back of the house where his father had converted one of the old bedrooms into his home office. When he arrived at the French glass doors, images of his father sitting in his leather chair behind the massive, shiny wooden desk came to mind. Over the past few years, whenever he visited his father, most of their time was spent in the office unless Mason brought food. And in that case, they'd eat in the dining room, then head to the office.

Pain filled his chest. His heart ached at the memories, yet he smiled, encouraged to cherish the time he shared with his father. Layla placed a soft hand on his shoulder. And though meant to comfort him, her touch released a range of emotions. He inhaled slowly, filling his chest with as much air as possible and slowly released.

Going through his father's things had to be done at some point, especially since he planned to sale the house, but now he searched because he wanted to find answers.

Mason twisted the knob. With heavy steps, he inched inside and flipped on the light switch. He placed the box on a side table. Layla intertwined her fingers in one of his free hands and squeezed. She didn't say anything, only gave what he'd consider a reassuring smile. This was tough for him. She knew it. He knew it. And while being there wasn't necessary, he was grateful for the compassion she showed, allowing him to take things slow.

The office smelled of cedar pine and a mix of his father's cologne. His father's desk was clean as always, with only his calendar and closed laptop on the surface. Degrees and awards hung on the walls, along with an old wooden grandfather clock his father refused to get rid of because it was a gift from his wife. Never mind the fact that the pendulum didn't work, he couldn't part with it. And now that his father was gone, Mason understood holding on to things that reminded a person of those they loved most.

He walked over to the desk and picked up his father's laptop. The tufted leather sofa was a better seating choice than his father's leather chair behind the desk. Mason couldn't bring himself to sit there. He settled on the sofa with Layla next to him. She rested her hand on his shoulder while he flipped open the laptop and keyed in his father's password, which was Mason's name spelled with symbols and numbers.

On the desktop screen was a file labeled *Congressional Race*. His heart slammed in his chest. What if this file was the missing link, the key to finding the answers he needed to get the closure he desperately craved? He turned to his left, locking eyes with Layla who rested her chin on the hand that comforted his shoulder. Though they often sat close when working together, this moment was different. Her being there meant everything to him. Her kissable lips were mere centimeters away, drawing his attention from the task at hand.

He couldn't help himself.

He didn't want to.

Mason leaned closer and whispered against her lips. "Thank you."

She held his gaze and didn't back away. Instead, her lips moved against his when she said, "You're welcome."

He couldn't respond verbally because she'd officially closed whatever limited space that was left between them. Her hand had moved from his shoulder to behind his neck, tugging him closer, as he relived the moment from their first kiss. There was no denying the fact that the woman felt good in his arms.

A kiss was a kiss, right? Technically, he wasn't experiencing fireworks or anything like that, but what he did realize was that they were indeed emotionally connected. And that's what made him want to kiss her every day for the rest of his life.

Mason broke the kiss with that thought.

Layla gave him a reassuring smile and used her thumb to massage away her lipstick, which smudged on his lips. She nodded toward the laptop as if to say it was okay for him to click on the folder he'd forgotten about when she kissed him.

When Mason double-clicked the folder, over one hundred items appeared, a combination of photos, PDFs, and Word documents. He took the opportunity to click through each one, beginning with the first item and worked his way down to the last file.

Photos of his father and other businessmen, a couple of whom were also running for congress, were in the files. Some of the documents appeared to be the electronic copy of what he and Layla pulled from the ottoman in his father's man cave. He even saw photos of his father and the congresswoman, who he felt was responsible in some way. Mason just needed to prove it.

"Since your father is also in some of these photos, do you think someone sent these to him?"

Mason nodded. "Someone sending these to him would make more sense and also mean that maybe he was being threatened, possibly to pull out of the race. Why wouldn't he tell me something like this, though?"

"I don't know your father, but like most dads, he probably figured he had the situation under control. Plus, I'm sure he'd want to protect you."

"*Hmmmph.* Sounds like you did know him."

Layla shrugged. She'd put her hand back on his shoulder and squeezed. "I'm just thinking about how I believe my dad would respond in the same situation. Either way, I feel like we're getting close. Much closer than we have been."

"Me, too. I can't put my finger on it, but something feels different now. Let's go back to the office and cross reference what we have here with what we received from Detective Mansfield's thumb drive. I'm sure there's a connection somewhere. I'm not going to rest tonight until I find it."

Layla looked at him as if he'd grown another head. Yes, he was serious about staying up late to figure this thing out. She shouldn't be surprised.

Mason closed the laptop and unplugged the charger. "Hey, I'm not trying to impose on your personal time. Me staying up late doesn't mean you have to do so. I'll be working through this long after office hours and will catch you up in the morning."

She moved her chin back to the hand that rested on his shoulder. "You should know by now that you aren't in this alone. If you're staying up, so am I."

While he valued her tenacity, Mason trusted himself less and less in her company. "Let's just see how much we can uncover during the rest of the afternoon."

Layla offered one of those you-aren't-going-to-get-rid-of-me smiles. "Deal."

What she didn't understand was that this was the fight of his life in more ways than one. He had to find out what really happened to his father and expose the political misconduct in their city, which at this juncture, he hoped would lead him to answers about the COO's murder as well. He couldn't prove it yet, but they were all linked. And he had to do all of that while keeping his growing emotions for her under control. So, yes, even though being with her made his world spin on the right axis, he couldn't fully act on his feelings for her and move forward until they'd done the job.

CHAPTER SEVENTEEN

L ayla needed the alone time to decompress after being with Mason in his father's house for the last couple of hours. She'd confirmed that kissing him was special. Something terrifying, but also exciting happened inside of her when their lips touched. Her body warmed and her heartbeat escalated to this crazy tempo. She felt out of control in a way she'd never experienced. In the midst of digging through documents, kissing him was a nice distraction from the dread looming over her resulting from the nightmare and learning of possible foul play surrounding Walter Sterling's death.

She trailed him back to the office. Even being one car space away from him, she still felt his presence. Or more so the imprint of his lips against hers. And what a good memory that was. She licked her lips then ran her finger along the bottom. What was she going to do about this man?

Pull it together. You can't be distracted.

Thirty minutes later, they parked in the downtown parking garage nearest their office building. She hadn't even had time to cut her engine and grab her purse before Mason was at her driver's side door. With the file box in one hand, he opened her door with the other. She doubted he'd admit it, but this ongoing case was wearing away at him. While looking into the congresswoman and her son, he wasn't prepared for the possibility of her being linked to his father's death. He needed answers, but he also dreaded what he would find. Or at least she did. Her heart ached for him. Things like this were never easy, and who was to say that what they found wouldn't untangle a deeper web of secrets and lies than it already had? Were they ready for that?

Ready or not, they had to push forward.

Layla stepped out of the car. "Thanks."

"You're welcome."

On their walk to their office, Layla asked, "Do you think we need to update Simon on what we found in the dossiers of the congressional candidates?"

"I don't normally talk to him much about my assignments unless I run into a problem, and that's only been twice in my career. Once I received a cease-and-desist letter from the Texas Department of Family and Protective Services in an effort to block me from publishing a story about child abuse that they believed was confidential. We would never cite the names of any children, nor were we intending to do so, and all the information I received was obtained legally, so that letter didn't stop me from publishing the story. However, I was surprised when the letter came in the mail. Plus, with that being my very first case, I was nervous about it, but I've learned since then that there will always be someone who opposes what I do and will threaten to induce bodily harm or pursue monetary damages to get me to stop my research and publishing."

"Wow."

"I know. The second instance I spoke to Simon about a case was when you walked in and heard a piece of our conversation."

Layla looked up at him with scrunched eyebrows. She could only imagine how distorted her features looked in the moment. "Seriously?"

They'd made it inside the building, and Mason pressed the elevator call button. "Yes, seriously."

She withdrew into her thoughts while they claimed the next elevator and rode it to their floor. And Mason hadn't said anything else, which made her believe he wanted her to think through her question and decide how to proceed. His responses were often given in such a way to encourage her to make decisions on her own. She appreciated his coaching and training style.

When they arrived at their cubicles, Layla stuffed her purse into the filing cabinet under her desk. Mason placed the box down on his desk and sat in his chair facing her. "So, what do you want to do? Feel like talking to Simon?"

Layla powered on her laptop while she considered his question. While having another person help them think through what they'd found out so far would be great, she needed to wrap her head around the facts and not simply speculation. "Let's wait until we can cross reference what we found in those files and thumb drive with what we recovered from Detective Mansfield. Agreed?"

"Yes. Fine by me."

Mason sifted through the files and spread them across his desk area. He copied the files from the thumb drive he'd secured from his father's house, then handed it to Layla to do the same.

"We found ten dossiers at your dad's house. I can take the first five, and you can take the second half. I'll see if there's anything I can find in the information we already have that could somehow tie them to what Detective Mansfield was investigating. I truly believe there's a link there that will help us narrow this list. Does that work for you?"

Mason gave her one of those I'm-so-proud-of-you-that-I-can-kiss-you smiles and handed her five dossiers. At least that's the way she received the way he looked at her. "Sounds good."

Layla gave Mason a gentle nod before sliding her chair in front of her laptop screen. They'd spent so much time together in her cubicle space, it felt odd not having him next to her for them to go through the documents side by side. While a part of her wanted to change the plan and suggest they work through each dossier together, their time would be better and more efficiently spent by splitting the task as they agreed.

She flipped open the first file. Congresswoman Lackey. Her photo was clipped to the first page. Pretty woman. Blond hair. Pretty smile with a pair of brown eyes that couldn't be trusted. Mason already had his suspicions about her, which made Layla more critical when reading through her file. The poor woman couldn't receive the benefit of the doubt. Not from her. Layla had already glanced at the dossier back at Mason's father's house, but now that she had an opportunity to take a second and more detailed look, she couldn't believe the words on the page. A better question would be what had the congresswoman done right in her tenure. Bribes, shifting contracts to her preferred bidders, mismanaging political funds, embezzlement, destruction of mail-in ballots. The works.

Layla also read through whistleblower interviews, which she assumed was how the investigation into her began. Lavish trips using campaign funds. Altered documents, which when compared with the original documents, showed the trail of her embezzlement from funds intended for charity but ended up in her offshore bank accounts.

Layla began her search through Detective Mansfield's files. *Would Detective Mansfield have been investigating you?*

She'd clicked the keypad so much in the last couple of hours that her index finger stiffened. There were photos of Lackey with other businessmen. Then there was a file extension with her name. When Layla opened it, it was more of the same information she read in the dossier.

She moved on to the next file. Sidney Matthews. Much like the information she'd read about Lackey, his was more of the same, except he wasn't a politician. He owned True Technology Industries. He and Congresswoman Lackey were connected in that she'd pushed a government contract his way. And according to the documents, giving the bid to him didn't make fiscal sense, given his bid was higher than all other bidders involved.

Her head pounded like a jackhammer, and she wasn't even halfway through her stack. Layla massaged her temples. "Mason."

He pushed away from his cubicle and turned to face her. "What's up? Find something?"

That accent of his would send her heart teetering if she wasn't focused. "I've realized something. Shouldn't the FBI be investigating these people? I mean, this seems above anything Detective Mansfield would be involved in. It's just not making sense."

"The thought has crossed my mind because I haven't been able to wrap my head around it, either. I also don't understand why any of this would be in my dad's possession, and why would he hide it from me?"

She tapped the files. "These are some serious crimes. I can understand why he wouldn't mention it. For all we know, the FBI could be investigating these people, and your dad could've been helping them as an informant."

Mason frowned. "My pops wasn't a snitch."

He was clearly offended. And while she liked to tread carefully when discussing his father, Walter Sterling being an FBI informant was the only thing that made sense right now. Why else would he have all of that information? And how did he get it?

Layla took a deep breath and spoke in the voice she'd used over the years to manage upset employees. "I'm not calling your father names, Mason, but would you just consider the possibility for a moment? Maybe this started out as something Detective Mansfield was working on as part of another case, and once she found out about the political corruption, she got the FBI involved."

"While I don't like the idea of my father being an informant, I do like your theory. If Congresswoman Lackey knew about the feds and had reason to believe my dad was helping the FBI, it would make sense that she knew my dad had information on others involved, including her—or at least she suspected he did."

"Sounds like we know what we need to do."

"Yeah." Mason stood and stuffed files and his laptop into his backpack. "I'm going home to comb through my dad's e-mails and thumb drive. There has to be something there."

Images of Mason's lifeless body lying on the concrete in front of that convenience store in the middle of the night fog plagued her thoughts. Layla jumped out of her seat and stuffed her portfolio bag with files and her laptop. He would not leave her behind to follow a trail that would lead to his death. Not if she could help it. "What can I do?"

"Stay on track with what you're working on. Look for a connection in the files."

That almost sounded like he was trying to dismiss her.

"Text me your address. I'll grab dinner and head over."

∞

Layla had fully inserted herself into the situation. To be fair, she was doing what Simon paid her to do—work. However, inviting herself over to his home was not in her job description. She stood there with her defiant chin tilted upward as if she dared him to say she couldn't come over.

She smiled like she had the upper hand. "No fuss, Mason. We already agreed that we'd work late together."

Given the level of chemistry between them, they should work late in the office, but the air conditioner shut off at six, so office work was not an option after quitting time. A restaurant was also a possibility, but he really just wanted to go home, get comfortable in his favorite pair of sweats and work until he pieced together this puzzle.

Mason closed the space between them, leaned over, and spoke with his lips close to her ear so that no one else could hear. Not that it mattered because their cubicles were in the back of the office and the nearest journalist was at least fifty feet away. The scent he'd associated as uniquely Layla, powdery with a soft floral fragrance, crept up his nose. He inhaled softly before he said, "Are you sure it's a good idea for you to be alone with me again?"

He backed away and observed her eyes, which answered *no,* but her mouth said, "Of course. We're so close to figuring this out that *nothing* else will cross our minds." The dramatic rise and fall of her chest further proved what he knew to be true. This was a terrible idea, but he'd be on his best behavior. No more kissing her—at least until after this story was published and he'd gotten justice for his father.

"Okay." Mason pulled his phone from his pocket. He chuckled while he typed his address along with a message that read, *I know you find it hard to resist me, but please do so tonight so we can get our work done.*

Layla's phone vibrated. "Sounds like I've got your message." She whipped out her phone to check. "I'll call you when I'm on my way." Seconds later, she laughed out loud. "You wish."

168

Mason laughed along with her. "I know you're not ready to admit the truth just yet. I understand. C'mon. I'll walk you to your car."

After seeing Layla safely to her vehicle, Mason hopped into his own and spent the drive processing the new direction of their investigation. The whole idea of his father being an FBI informant was insane to consider, yet made sense. But if that were true, he was even more upset because the FBI should have protected him. He shouldn't have had to bury his father months ago. Didn't the FBI protect their informants?

When he arrived home, he washed the day off and slipped into his favorite pair of gray sweatpants with his alma mater's acronym on one pant leg and one of his tattered alumni t-shirts to match. He clicked on the television and pressed play on one of his streaming apps just to have white noise in the background. Layla still hadn't called, but he didn't plan to wait around on her to get started.

He made himself comfortable on his dark brown leather sofa and reclined. The remote and his cell phone rested on the arm. His soda was in the center console while the laptop was in his lap.

Mason picked up his research where he left off back in the office. Donovan Finch. While he wasn't a politician, Mason's dad introduced him as one of Houston's prominent businessmen at his father's fundraiser. From what Mason remembered, and based on the dossier, Donovan owned a real estate business that focused on renovating Houston, which was how Donovan described his

169

business venture. Finch Real Estate Solutions' primary goal was to renovate the homes of senior citizens to give them a better life.

Though Mason didn't talk to Donovan for long, he didn't get the feeling that anything was off about the man or that he had some sort of hidden agenda. But based on what Mason read in the dossier, he should be concerned about Donovan. Over the past three years, Finch Real Estate Solutions received grants from the government to help fulfill its mission of renovating homes, but nothing had been done. In fact, the man hadn't renovated a single home in the past four years, but had somehow qualified for and received grants for the last three years.

Was Donovan trying to get in his father's good graces to keep his good thing going?

Layla's call interrupted his thoughts.

"Hey, change your mind?" he teased.

"And ruin your evening because you find it hard to work without me? Never."

Mason burst into laughter. "Always with the jokes."

Layla chuckled. "Just call it like I see it. Anyway, I'm about to pick up salmon from Goode Seafood. Does that work for you?"

"Sounds really good, actually. About what time do you think you'll get here?"

"When we get off the phone, I'll call to place an order for pick-up, so it should be ready by the time I get there. So, maybe another thirty–forty minutes. Will you be able to make it without me for forty more minutes?" She laughed.

"I will do my best."

"Bye. See you in a bit."

Mason shook his head when they ended the call. His chest expanded because Layla had this way of making his world seem a little less sad. And if God sent her into his life to help him get through this difficult time, then he owed Him a round of praise.

In the meantime, his growling stomach kept him company while he waited for his coworker guest to arrive with their dinner. And so did the files before him. The one thing that was missing or that he couldn't understand was the tie between Donovan and Detective Mansfield. How did she fit into the puzzle? Was she truly killed because someone—one of these people—thought she'd passed him information that could incriminate them? And even more so, why would she be investigating political corruption?

Mason cross-referenced her notes and files to see if there was anything about Donovan Finch or his company that would connect him to Detective Mansfield. There were hundreds of files from Detective Mansfield's thumb drive. Photos of Donovan and his father. Photos of Donovan and other businessmen. And photos of Donovan and other politicians. Mason's best guess was that Detective Mansfield wasn't investigating any of these people, but was given the storage device. And if his hunch was correct, then who would give the device to her and why?

He'd discuss his theory with Layla after she arrived, and they'd had an opportunity to eat. That way, they could think straight. He hit the side key on his phone to check the time and saw a text from her: *On my way.* That was five minutes ago. His stomach rumbled in response.

He had at least another fifteen minutes before she'd be at his door, so he set his laptop aside and grabbed his father's laptop from the coffee table. *C'mon, Dad.* There had to be at least one e-mail with enough information to push him further along in this investigation.

Mason needed justice for his father and his story. Figuring out what the Congresswoman was up to would be the key to everything.

He logged into his dad's e-mail account, for which he didn't need a password because his father had his credentials saved. First, Mason skimmed his father's inbox, which it seemed he never deleted any e-mails. According to the message count, there were over ten thousand e-mails.

This is going to take all night.

But that was exactly what he planned to do—work all night. He expanded the inbox to show one hundred e-mails at a time and began skimming. Just as he settled into his task, his doorbell rang. Mason shoved his laptop to the side and ran to meet Layla at the door.

She'd changed clothes as well. He'd never seen her dressed as comfortably as she was standing on his doorstep in a pair of leggings and an oversized T-shirt. Holding a bag of food, she looked like an angel from heaven. He relieved her of the bag and stepped aside to let her. Her fresh scent overpowered the food. Or maybe it was just him. He'd memorized the smell of her and could smell her even when she wasn't around.

He had it bad.

CHAPTER EIGHTEEN

It was time Layla stopped denying how attracted she was to Mason. She was only lying to herself anyway. Even dressed in a pair of sweatpants and faded t-shirt, the man stirred something within her that made her want to throw herself into her arms and kiss him again. And again. She'd never been that type of person before now. The type who dreamed about kissing. The type who desired it. Or the type who felt like she couldn't go too long without it.

But it wasn't just about the kiss.

It was Mason.

She stepped inside of his townhouse and followed him into the kitchen. There was little color in the house. The walls were natural almond. Chocolate leather furniture. Black appliances. Aside from the large flat-screen television that hung on the wall, there was only one photo of his mother and father. She only knew that because she'd observed a similar picture at his father's house. He led her to a small breakfast table in the dining area right off the kitchen. Mason slid the chair out for her before removing the food from the bag.

"What would you like to drink?"

"I'll take soda if you have one, otherwise, bottled water is fine."

Mason disappeared behind her into the kitchen. Layla continued observing her surroundings. His home was clean, but based on what she saw, there wasn't much opportunity for it to be messy. Or maybe he'd thrown all of his dirty laundry on the floor in his bedroom upstairs. But she didn't take Mason to be the messy type. He'd shown himself to be a simple, no-fuss kind of guy.

He returned to the table with two glasses filled with ice and two soda cans. "Here you go." When he sat, he reached for her hands, bowed his head, and led them in a quick prayer of thanks.

"Amen," Layla said after he closed the prayer.

"You came right on time because I am starving."

Layla nodded and cut a piece of salmon with her fork. "Yeah, I know. If I hadn't shown up, you'd probably work right through dinner." She took a bite.

"Nah, I would have grabbed something eventually, even if it was just a protein shake."

"Stop doing that to yourself. I've noticed a pattern with you. When you're focused, you will work right through lunch unless I suggest we go. You have to take better care of yourself, Mason."

While he chewed his food, he looked at her in a way that made her believe he reciprocated whatever feelings she had for him. He smiled, and she could see the range of emotions pass through his eyes. But he didn't address them. "I think I do a pretty good job of taking care of myself. I just feel like we're really close to getting answers, and I'm determined to get to the bottom of this. When I'm in the zone, work consumes me."

"I see. So, tell me about your most memorable story, or better yet, your favorite in your career."

He scooped another forkful of salmon in his mouth and thought while he chewed. "It would have to be a story I never got the opportunity to finish. And some parts of this investigation remind me of it. I was away in Washington to investigate political favors and financial crimes. The story was and is a deep dive into the illegal operation to spy on a former treasury public figure by bugging the home of another former public official. I can't cite names because the investigation is still ongoing. When my mother got sick three years ago, I left the assignment to come home and be with her."

"I understand. Seems there's plenty of political corruption going around."

"Yeah. When we're deep in an investigation, I know it can feel that way. Makes the politicians who are doing what they're supposed to do look bad, too."

Layla finished up her food and closed the container. "Agreed."

"We've never really talked about how you're feeling about this job. Think you'll stick around for a while, or are you secretly planning to get away from me as soon as possible?"

Layla threw her head back and laughed.

Mason chuckled. "Laughing like that makes me believe you can't wait to leave us and go back to Langston Brands."

"Actually, it's just the opposite. I don't want to leave you. I've found my place and am exactly where I should be. Every assignment will be different, and I look forward to the adventures of each one."

"I take that to mean I'm an excellent coach and mentor. Be sure you use those words when you talk to Simon."

Laughter bubbled from her belly. "If I lay the compliments on too thick, Simon will see right through me."

In fact, Simon wasn't blind. Layla would bet that at the very least, Simon suspected she and Mason had a thing for each other, even if he didn't know the extent of their fondness. And maybe it was because of the relationship he had with Mason or because he'd known all that Mason had lost in the last couple of years, but Simon didn't seem bothered as far as she could ascertain.

"You're right. He'll probably accuse me of telling you to say those things."

"You two seem to have a good working relationship. Do you ever hang out with him outside of work?"

Mason nodded. He shifted in his seat, leaned forward, with his elbows on the table. "Simon is the only person I'd call a friend. We met in college, but he is two years my senior. After he graduated, he went to work. Me, on the other hand, I served four years in the army. When I left the army, Simon had advanced to editor-in-chief *at The Houston Exposure*. That's when he reached out to me to see if I was interested in the job, and I've been here since."

"Wow. So what was that, six to seven years to get to editor-in-chief? That's fast, isn't it? How'd he manage that?"

"He works hard, but *The Houston Exposure* was also founded by his family."

"Say no more. You know I understand how that goes. I came from a family-run business."

"Product of nepotism."

Layla chuckled. "I cannot disagree with you there. My path would've been quite different if my family's expectations weren't for me and my sisters to run the business after we finished college. See? There are disadvantages to nepotism. Who knows? I could've been here years ago imposing on your cases."

A soft chuckle escaped his lips, but his features turned serious. His focus was intense enough to make her squirm. "While that's true, I'm sure I need you more now than I would have at any other point in my life. God's timing is always perfect."

"Always."

Need you?

Layla cleared her throat. She couldn't delve deep into serious personal conversation. They were supposed to keep things light and focus on their research.

"Since you made me promise to resist you, we'd better end this discussion and get to work."

∞

Mason couldn't help but laugh. If nothing else, he enjoyed every second he spent with Layla, no matter what they were doing. He stood and reached for her hand. "C'mon. I'm set up in the living room. Before you showed up, I'd just started going through my dad's e-mails."

"Oh, I left my portfolio bag with my laptop and files in my trunk."

"Unlock the door, and I'll run out to grab it for you."

He led her to the sofa where she sat next to the spot he'd occupied earlier. The dash to her car took less than two minutes. When he came back inside the house, her eyes were glued to one of the files he'd been going through earlier. Mason sat next to her and handed over the leather portfolio bag.

"Have you found anything in the e-mails?"

Mason shook his head. "He has over ten thousand messages. I'm not even close—at least I don't think so."

"Good luck with that. I can help once I'm done with these files. You know, based on what I read in those dossiers earlier, I don't think Detective Mansfield was doing any investigation. I truly believe someone gave her those files, but I can't figure out why."

Mason sighed. "Yeah, I can't reconcile that either. Although, she did mention she and my dad were friends, which was news to me, but it's not like I kept up with everyone he was connected to."

Layla turned to him. "So, are you thinking your dad may have given the files to her?"

"The thought crossed my mind, but then that wouldn't make sense if we go with the theory that he was an FBI informant. Why would the local police be involved?"

"She could've been involved in some type of special joint task force assisting with the investigation. I mean, she was local and would've had more knowledge about these businessmen involved. It's not far-fetched."

Mason shifted his weight on the sofa so that he faced her. The center console separated them. "I can get with that. So, let's think through this. My dad, an informant, and Detective Mansfield, part of the FBI special joint task force investigating the corruption. After my dad died in that explosion, she assumed someone might come after her, too. That explains why she passed us the files."

"But did she not trust the FBI to finish the job?"

"No, I think it's the opposite. She wanted to ensure all their dirty deeds were exposed, and she knew I wouldn't stop until I found the answers."

Layla fist bumped him. "We're such a good team. I think we should come up with a team name."

Mason laughed out loud at the thought of a team name. "Too much."

Layla chuckled. "Don't worry. I'll workshop it."

"You're not allowed to think about a team name until we finish this investigation and story. Now let's see if there's something in these e-mails that can help prove our theory. If not, the next best solution would be to befriend one of them, gain their trust, and see what they'll tell us. And that would likely have to be you. I don't think any of them will want to be my friend, unless they thought I was running for office and could somehow assist them in their criminal efforts."

"What? Who wouldn't want to be Mason Sterling's friend?"

"You're joking, but I'm serious. Everyone knows what I do. They'll suspect I'm running game on them, but they won't see your pretty face coming."

Layla blushed. "I know what you're doing, and it's working, so stop it." She pointed to the laptop in his lap. "Focus on those e-mails."

Mason smirked. He enjoyed being the reason the small dimple on her right cheek showed itself. When it came to Layla, he couldn't help himself. The energy between the two of them was magnetic. And the more he tried to resist the pull, the closer they became. If it weren't for the console separating them, he would have pulled her close and kissed that dimple. He shook his head to dismiss the thought. They had work to do, and he wouldn't get anywhere thinking about things he liked about her.

For the next two hours, they worked in silence with the only sound coming from the movie playing on his streaming service. Mason focused on his dad's e-mails while Layla read through dossiers and took notes. His eyes grew tired and crossed looking at the computer screen. Thousands of e-mails about his father's real estate business, which was to be expected. His father owned a local real estate franchise. But not one thing about the people in question. Mason had even run a search using each of the names in the dossiers. Nothing.

He huffed and stood to stretch his legs. "I'm getting nowhere, and it's frustrating." Mason rubbed the back of his neck and paced the floor. He had to be missing something.

Layla looked up at him with a gleam in her eyes—a gleam that halted his pacing.

"What is it?"

She turned her laptop screen toward him and pointed to a note that had been scribbled on a scanned document. "The Gathering." Mason shrugged. "Unless I'm missing something, that doesn't tell me anything."

Layla shook her head. "I'm beginning to wonder how you've made it this far in your career without me."

Mason chuckled as he reclaimed his seat. He opened his palms for the laptop. "Give me that." For a few minutes, he read the page Layla had on her screen. "So, that's what they call themselves? The Gathering?"

"Right, which also means that we were right. All ten people in the dossiers we found are working together. And whatever they're doing now is probably their biggest scheme yet."

Mason handed the laptop back to Layla and searched "The Gathering" in his father's e-mail account. No e-mails, only a calendar entry for later that evening.

"I think we've just found ourselves a party."

Layla craned her neck to look at his screen. "What party?"

Mason turned his laptop to face her. "There's a gathering tonight at nine. I doubt it's a coincidence. Whatever is happening, it seems my dad was planning to attend, and since he can't attend, we should go check it out."

A mix of emotions flashed through her features, one of which he identified as terror, but that was strange considering she'd been adamant about seeing this investigation through to story publication. However, she pasted on a smile, and not the kind of smile that he was used to seeing on her face. This one made him believe she was hiding something from him. Was it a dream she hadn't shared with him? "Let's do it."

There was no time to sit around and discuss her dreams. He'd ask her about it on the way to this meeting scheduled to start in the next hour.

CHAPTER NINETEEN

Layla's stomach had burst into tiny knots and tumbled around inside her body. Over and over again. And if the gyration in her belly wasn't warning enough, sweat beads formed on the back of her neck and rolled down her back. Not a good combination with the leather seats in Mason's truck. Before long, her sweat soaked shirt would have her stuck to the seat like her mind and lips seemed to be. Stuck. Stuck with fear. Was her nightmare coming to fruition? It was now dark. And the more they drove, the foggier it became. She repeated slow inhales and exhales to calm her nerves.

Mason took his eyes off the road for a second and glanced at her. "You okay?"

She bobbed her head up and down. *"Ummm-hmmm."*

Her heartbeat escalated despite her efforts to relax.

"Are you sure? Because I'm not getting okay vibes from you. Do you have something you want to tell me?"

How do you even tell someone you had a nightmare they would be murdered and that the present was unfolding much like what you saw in your REM sleep? *If you care about him, you'll say something.*

"Can you pull over?"

Mason hiked an eyebrow, surely not wanting to waste time. He had to be driving at least seventy miles per hour. But he must have sensed the worry in her voice or maybe saw it in her face. He took the next exit and slowed his truck to a stop at a gas station and shifted the gear into park. Even the gas station looked familiar.

We're already here.

She swallowed the knot in her throat.

He covered her trembling hands with his. Almost like magic, the move stilled her nerves, but her heart continued on like it was on a mission to get out of her chest as soon as possible.

"Let me guess. You saw some version of this in a dream, and I got hurt? Am I on the right track?"

She nodded. The movement caused tears to spill from her eyes. "You were killed." She spoke with a low voice. The words pained her to utter. And the proof was in the way her throat hurt.

Mason squeezed her hand.

Silence passed between them while the digits on the dashboard's clock ticked on for another minute. Finally, he asked, "So what do you want me to do?"

Turn around and go back home. Stay as far away from this dark part of town as possible. Stay away from these people. Find another way. But he wouldn't hear any of those things. They'd come too far.

"Stay inside the truck."

Mason shrugged. "That's easy enough if that's all it will take to keep me alive."

184

"I don't feel like you're taking this seriously."

"I can't promise that I'll stay inside, especially when I don't know what we're running into. If there's an opportunity to get inside to hear what's going on, I have to take it."

Her voice raised an octave. "No, you don't. You don't have to do anything."

"You seem to have forgotten why we're here, Layla. We're here to get answers, and for me, that's whatever it takes." Mason didn't raise his voice, but it became stern. The softness with which he usually spoke to her was now absent.

"And for me, that's whatever it takes within reason. I don't want to lose you, Mason."

He shifted in his seat and looked her in the eye—the first time he'd looked her in the face since they started this conversation. "I care about you, too, Layla. Don't worry about me. I know how to handle myself. Just know that I'll be careful, okay?"

Tucking his hand behind her head, he pulled her close and murmured against her lips, "Come here."

All kinds of emotions swirled within her when his lips met hers. Comfort. Fear. Satisfaction. Joy. Anxiety. Yet, she savored the moment, not knowing if it would be her last and she'd find herself crouched over him begging him to breathe and not leave her. But that nightmare wasn't real. She had to have faith.

Mason broke the kiss first and murmured against her lips again, "It'll all be okay."

The back of her neck felt cold when his hand was back on the gear shift. He nodded, and she returned the gesture. When he shifted the gear into drive, she released a slow breath, which she intended to calm her nerves, but the truth was that she wouldn't be calm until they returned to his home—safe and away from this possible drama.

When Mason navigated his truck back onto the road, they were about five minutes from their destination. They arrived and parked at a distance. Mason shut off his headlights. From their line of vision, they could see anyone who parked in the lot and crossed the street to go inside the building.

It was dark and foggy like her dream, but the area wasn't as familiar. She hadn't noticed a convenience store unless it was around the corner. The building they were watching sat on the corner, so she didn't know what was on the street behind it. And she couldn't bring herself to open the map app on her phone only to confirm there indeed was a convenience store there. This was one of those moments where she wished she didn't have any dreams at all.

"How long has it been since you had the vision of me getting killed?"

Mason's question startled her. She'd been too busy trying to convince herself the present wasn't following her dream/nightmare sequence.

She shrugged. "I'm not sure. A week or two maybe."

"We agreed you'd tell me if you had any more dreams. Why didn't you trust me enough to tell me?"

Layla had to take a moment to calm herself again. "It wasn't that I didn't trust you. I just didn't know how to tell you. Honestly, that dream scared me, and if anything, I wanted to prevent it from happening. Like I said, I can't and don't want to lose you, Mason. Can you understand that?"

A bout of silence passed between them.

"I do, but I also don't want you to feel like you have to preserve my feelings. Please speak freely around me. I thought I'd made that clear. No judgment here."

"I get it, but are you telling me it wouldn't freak you out if someone told you they had a dream you were murdered right in front of them?"

"I'd be unnerved for a moment, but I'd also remember that it's just a dream and assume there was some other meaning other than my death."

"Well, let me rephrase that: If I walked into the office or called your cell and told you something like that, what would've been your reaction?"

Mason quirked an eyebrow. "I guess we'll never know."

Him and that accent. Those eyes. Lips. The strength of his mind. How his arms felt wrapped around her. The way he made her feel. Appreciated. Seen. Cared for. And it wasn't that she hadn't felt those things from another man before, but none of those men were Mason. He riled her up and calmed her at the same time. His energy. Their chemistry. Unmatched.

As if the members of The Gathering had planned their synchronized arrival, they each parked in the lot, one by one. By the time one person parked and walked into the building, the next person arrived. That cycle continued until all members were inside the building.

"Well, at least we know the calendar entry was correct. It's safe to say that The Gathering is real, and they're up to something. But Layla, we won't get any answers sitting inside of this truck. We can't hear or see what's going on. We need eyes and ears inside of that building."

He spoke as if he was asking permission and trying to convince her. However, she knew he'd already decided not to stay in the car. And Layla the journalist agreed that their trip would be for nothing if they didn't get close enough to hear what was happening. But Layla the woman who cared about Mason the man didn't agree. She couldn't lose him. They'd hardly begun to know each other.

Defeated, she said, "You're right. But what's your plan? You can't be reckless."

"When am I ever reckless?"

Layla folded her arms across her chest. "And now isn't the time to start. So, what's your plan?"

Mason canvassed their surroundings. "The building is right across the street. Based on our count, every member of The Gathering is already inside. I'll just stand at the door to listen in. That's it."

Confused, Layla asked, "How are you going to listen through the door?"

Mason reached behind Layla's seat and pulled out a small black backpack. He unzipped it and removed an electronic device she couldn't identify. "With this."

"What is that thing?"

"An amplifier. It'll allow me to listen through the door as long as it isn't made of concrete, which I'm fairly certain it isn't, so we're good."

Layla had to trust Mason knew what he was doing and that he'd keep himself safe. Perhaps this situation wouldn't play out the way her dream slash nightmare had if she stayed inside the truck. Though it was dark, she had enough light to where she'd see his movements in the shadows.

"Okay. You've got this," she said more to convince herself than to encourage him.

He gave that confident nod before he climbed out of the truck, removed a weapon from his backpack and secured it to his waist. "Everything will be fine. Stay in the truck and keep watch."

Lord, please don't let him die. I love him.

∞

Mason hustled across the street. Trepidation tore through him with each step. This wasn't his first rodeo, but Layla's nightmare bothered him. And the fact that her dreams were foretelling shook him just a little. But he couldn't tell her that. He wouldn't. Finding answers was the job. They both knew that. And sometimes danger came along with the territory. He had to leave this earth one day, but he didn't want that to be today, so he would do everything in his power to be safe while also making sure he did the job.

Layla's words replayed in his mind: *I don't want to lose you.* And after finding someone he cared for more than anyone in his past, he'd do his best to get back to her. He didn't want to lose her either. In fact, he wanted the opposite.

To see her every day.

To keep getting to know her past this assignment, although future assignments would take them in different directions.

He didn't want different paths. What Mason desired was Layla by his side working through scenarios and writing stories together from here on out.

I should've told her how I feel.

He hated leaving words unsaid, but she'd caught him by surprise. While feelings for her crept up on him, he wasn't quite ready to share them. And because this emotional experience was new to him, he didn't have the words to describe what was happening in his heart. Well, that was a lie. He loved her, but they weren't anywhere near the place in their friendship—because they weren't in a committed relationship—to profess any sort of feelings. Mason rubbed a palm over his face. Now wasn't the time to think about any of that stuff. He had to get his head in the game.

Heavy fog lingered in the atmosphere. From where he stood near the door, he could see his truck parked in the lot across the street, and that was probably because he knew it was there. The rest of his surroundings were difficult to make out.

The area was secluded. Nearby buildings appeared abandoned or were businesses that closed by sundown. His target sat on the corner, and Mason didn't have much of a visual beyond the stop sign. He looked over his shoulder before he climbed three concrete steps that led to an enclosed entry. The door didn't appear to be heavy duty, which was great in his opinion.

He leaned his ear toward the door panel, placed the microphone on the door, and turned the amplifier on to the lowest setting. At first the voices came through scrambled, but that only lasted a few seconds. When clear, he turned up the sound a little, took a deep breath, and listened. He prayed this would help him discover the truth about his father's death and shed a light on the political corruption happening in their city.

The people inside were speaking in low voices, but Mason could hear every word, thanks to the amplifier.

A woman's voice asked, "So, where are we with getting funding for our project?"

A man answered, "We should be good to go. Lackey has promised she'll do what it takes to get the project approved."

"But how long will that take? And how can we trust her? She's been talking to Sterling's son. How do we know she isn't also working with the FBI?"

"Haven't I come through before?" Mason recognized the voice as Congresswoman Lackey's. "Have I also kept quiet about his murder? And the detective? What more do I need to do to prove myself to you, Donovan?"

Mason's heart plunged to his feet while anger rose within him. He clenched his fist hard enough to dig his nails into his palm. She confirmed what he suspected. His father's death was not an accident. A myriad of emotions tore through him, but he couldn't succumb to any of them. He smoothed a palm over his face and reset his focus.

And Donovan. Another name in the dossier.

The man raised his voice. Mason could tell he spoke through gritted teeth. "Now don't act like you're innocent in any of this. If we don't get the funding for this project, I won't hesitate to say you're behind the explosion that killed Sterling and sent your son to kill the detective. Let's not forget that your son's DNA is already in question for Flex Technology's COO's murder."

"Because of you. It's your DNA because of the blood transfusion."

"Happy to be his guardian angel. I saved his life so the least your family could do is protect mine."

"I ought to—"

"Be careful with your words, congresswoman. We wouldn't want you involved in an accident."

Someone slammed their hands on the table.

"Is that a threat?" Congresswoman Lackey's voice echoed through the amplifier.

"No, ma'am. It's a promise. We've come too far not to get what we want. Government funding is essential for the next phase in our project. The Gathering is built on one solid principle: Reform Houston."

Congresswoman Lackey's outburst continued. "Oh, give me a break. Let's be real. There's no one here but us. The only thing you want to reform is your business. You want to line your pockets. Who cares what happens to the projects in Houston? You'll come up with another excuse as to why the homes haven't been renovated, isn't that right?"

Another voice chimed in that Mason didn't recognize. "Let's all settle down. We want the same thing here, a better Houston and compensation for those who make it happen. We've already taken care of the FBI problem with Sterling out of the picture. Do we need to replace you, too, congresswoman? You're free to leave at any time."

The man spoke with such finality and coldness, a shiver ran through Mason. He hated the way they talked about his father as if he was some afterthought. Like he meant nothing. Well to them, he didn't mean anything. He was disposable. But for Mason, he was irreplaceable. The very thought made Mason's blood sizzle. He had to remain calm, so he took a deep breath to steady the heat rising within him.

Another woman's voice said, "What Jeffrey means is that now that Walter Sterling is no longer with us, congresswoman, you have nothing to worry about. We need you here. You're sort of like the glue that holds us all together. We believe in you, which is why we helped get you those votes you needed to remain in office. Everyone here believes you will do what it takes to help us make Houston a better place."

"Thank you, Camilla, but I know my worth, and what I also know is that killing Walter was not part of the plan. How do I know one of you won't get rid of me the moment I don't do what you want?"

Donovan's frustrated voice piped back in. "How about this? You will certainly be next if you don't do what we need you to do. Will that shut you up? Walter was never going to agree to any arrangement, and he was up in the polls. If he were still here, you would no longer be congresswoman, and our project would be over before it started. Trust me, whether you agree with his demise or not, you benefited from it."

Another man's voice cut through the argument. "Let's all get focused. Sterling is gone, and there's nothing we can do about that now. Let's all focus on our plan moving forward. Donovan, Lackey, can you two agree to get along for the greater good? We're all going to benefit when it's all said and done—fat pockets and a better Houston."

Even the calm of the man's voice bothered Mason. The promise he made to Layla was far behind him. Donovan was about to meet his Maker if Mason had any say so.

Mason stuffed the amplifier into the sling shoulder backpack. He turned to get a visual of his truck in the parking lot. As far as he could tell, Layla was still inside. Assured by that fact, he shifted the backpack so that it hung in its natural place over his shoulder. His blood boiled in his veins. He braced himself to burst through the door. Before he could complete the movement, a man about two inches taller than him appeared. In one swift movement, he inserted himself between Mason and the door and held his FBI badge in Mason's line of vision.

"And just what is your plan of action when you get inside?"

CHAPTER TWENTY

Everything happened faster than she could move. When Layla saw the man advancing toward Mason, she hesitated. Was her nightmare unfolding before her eyes? She couldn't make out what he was wearing, let alone whether he had a weapon. But he made it to Mason in one quick motion. Thankfully, there weren't any shots fired.

She breathed a sigh of relief. In fact, several sighs. She wasn't ready for a world without Mason, especially when they hadn't had their chance to be together—or at least for her to tell him she loved him.

When Mason's frame came into view, she halfway relaxed, if there was even such a thing. She watched to see what would happen next because everything seemed to be happening fast, yet slow. About five more men ran toward the building from the opposite direction of the parking lot where she sat in Mason's truck. Within seconds, they rushed inside. She assumed their vehicles were in another parking lot or that maybe they were parked alongside the curb. It was hard to tell given the heavy fog.

But all she cared about was Mason's safety. He moved to the side to make way for them. Were those guys FBI? That was the only thing that made sense. She wanted to climb out of the truck to get a sense of what was happening, but images of her nightmare came to mind. Would she be the reason Mason died if she left the truck and went to him? She couldn't risk it. She had to wait for him to come back and give her the details.

Something big was happening, and it bothered her to be so far away from the action. Layla whipped out her phone and flipped it between her fingers for about a minute. If she called Mason, he could tell her what was happening, but her call could also distract him.

However, she trusted him. He wouldn't answer her call if doing so would be a hindrance. She slid her fingers across the screen until his contact information appeared. Layla inhaled sharply, then released a controlled breath.

Lord, please let everything be okay. And please don't allow Mason to pick up the phone if this call will interfere with his wellbeing.

Confident that all would be well, Layla hit the telephone icon and waited. She watched his silhouette while the phone rang and rang. Layla then held her breath, remembering her prayer. Was something wrong?

Mason's frame faced the door, but he hadn't moved. His attention was focused on whatever was happening inside of the building. She saw him glance down at his pocket. Seconds later, he pulled his phone out and raised it to his ear.

"Hey. Are you okay?" he huffed through a heavy breath.

"Yeah, I'm good. Worried about you. I just saw about five men go inside the building. Were they FBI?"

"Yeah. This thing is crazy. Donovan killed my dad, and it's taking everything in me not to go in and take vengeance in my own hands."

"I'm sorry, Mason. What do you need me to do?"

"Please sit tight, and don't leave the truck."

"But—"

"Promise me you'll stay, Layla."

He knew her all too well. She was seconds away from climbing out of the truck to get to him. Not only did she need to know what was happening, she needed to make sure he was okay, but she relented, "Okay, but will you put me on speaker so that I can hear?"

Layla heard a bit of shuffling before he said, "I can't hold the phone right now, but you're now connected on my Bluetooth."

Now that she was in his ear hearing what he heard, she felt better. More like she was part of this investigation again, and part of the current happenings. Since he confirmed what happened to his father, maybe he'd also gained information about their political corruption, too. That had to be why the FBI stormed the building, right?

Shuffling and threats of calling lawyers rang through the phone followed by statements like, *You have the wrong person. I want my lawyer. You have no proof. We're being set up,* and *This is a waste of taxpayer dollars.*

Layla heard a man's stern voice say, "Now you care about taxpayer dollars? Where was all this concern when you were profiting from government contracts or pocketing charitable donations?"

"I've never done such a thing, and you have no proof of me committing any wrongdoing."

"How about you look right above the door and say hello." Based on his comment, Layla assumed there was a camera in the building. "Trust me, Mr. Donovan, we have all the information we need to put you and your friends where you belong for a very long time."

More grunting and statements of denial followed.

In a matter of seconds, five black full-sized SUVs pulled in front of the building, and one by one, each person in the dossiers, the members of The Gathering, were hauled out of the building in handcuffs and shoved into the backseats of the SUVs.

When the convoy vacated the area, Mason stood there with the FBI agent from earlier.

"I assume you have many questions, Mr. Sterling."

"And you'd be correct. Let's start with why you didn't protect my father from being murdered." His voice was cold and hard, nothing like the smooth voice she'd become accustomed to hearing.

Layla could no longer sit in the car. Mason had just confirmed his father was murdered, and the poor FBI agent would be on the receiving end of his bottled-up anger. Surely, he needed her right now.

She popped the lock and hopped out of the truck. "I'm coming, Mason."

Mason wasn't sure what burned him up more—Donovan's smug face when the FBI hauled him out in handcuffs or the FBI agent who stood there trying to manage him. He'd never been one who couldn't control his anger, but he wasn't sure how much longer that would be true. Mason flexed his hands and squeezed his fists repeatedly. Oh, if he could've wrapped his fingers around Donovan's throat for a few seconds, he might feel a little better. But that action wouldn't bring his father back nor honor his memory. Neither would his father want him to seek vengeance.

Maybe it was part of his training, but Mason despised the neutral face of the FBI agent.

"First, let me properly introduce myself. I'm Agent Chuck Williams. Your father and I were working closely together to bring down this ring of criminal politicians and businessmen who've been defrauding the government for years. They call themselves The Gathering."

Chuck Williams? Where had he heard that name before?

"And Agent Williams, I know you're smart enough to know that since I'm here and was listening in on their meeting, I have that information already. You still haven't answered my question. Why didn't you protect my father from being murdered? It doesn't make sense for you to swoop in here at just the right time to arrest those guys, but you couldn't keep my father safe. If you ask me, you and your team are fully responsible for his death."

"Now, hold on a minute."

"No." Mason stepped forward and pointed a finger in the man's face. "This is all on you." The more the scenario replayed in his mind, the more upset he became, but he wasn't crazy enough to assault a law enforcement officer.

Layla ran to his side. She stretched out her hand toward Agent Williams. "Hi. I'm Layla Langston. I work alongside Mason."

Agent Williams smiled for the first time that evening when he accepted Layla's handshake, and Mason didn't like the gesture, not one bit. "Nice to meet you, Layla."

Mason folded his arms across his chest and sized the man up. He didn't know what to make of Agent Williams or if he could be trusted. For all Mason knew, Agent Williams could be part of The Gathering, too. Maybe he pretended to raid the building and hauled them off to someplace safe.

"As I was just saying to Mr. Sterling, now that we have The Gathering in custody, I'm sure you all have more questions, and as I promised your father, I will answer anything that isn't classified, but this isn't the place to have this conversation. My team is in the van around the corner. If you'll follow me, we—"

Layla interrupted him. With one hip pushed to the side and her arms folded across her chest, she'd rolled her neck. "Agent Williams, I'm sorry, but I am not following you to a van, and I am not getting inside. It's dark and foggy. Sounds like a recipe to get chopped up and thrown in the Brazos River. Do you have any other recommendations because that's not happening?"

He chuckled. "I see how that can be alarming." He pressed his finger to his communication device in his ear. "Come around the front of the building. Layla and Mason need some reassurance."

Agent Williams stood with confidence and his hands stuffed into his pockets while they waited on his team.

"Agent Williams, there's nothing that will make us climb into that van with you. We can meet you somewhere, but that's about as close as we're going to get."

The agent smirked and faced the road.

About a minute later, a black van with Little Maria's Catering and a logo plastered on the side pulled to a stop in front of the curb. Mason reached behind him and placed his hand on his weapon. In all of his career, he hadn't needed to use it, but wouldn't hesitate if he had to.

Agent Williams held up a palm. "That's not necessary, Mason." He walked forward and slid open the van's side door and gestured inside. "As you can see, your father is alive and well."

CHAPTER TWENTY-ONE

Mason couldn't breathe.

His chest tightened, and he fought to get air out of his lungs and through his nose. Images of the past few months hurled at him at the speed of a freight train. He'd identified his father's body in the coroner's office. At the funeral home, he was the one who struggled through the process of making his father's final arrangements. The graveyard. His father's still, cold body. How could all of that have been a lie?

Layla grasped his hand while he worked to get a grip on what was real. He should be running to his father, squeezing his neck and thanking God his father wasn't dead, but Mason couldn't move. His conversation with Chief Gritlock replayed in his mind. Though the two of them never saw things the same, the chief seemed different the day he and Layla went to pay him a visit. And the more Mason thought about that conversation, he had to wonder if the chief knew his father was still alive.

Who else knew the truth?

Did Simon know?

Shoot, with all the dreams Layla had, did she know?

And how could his father allow him to grieve and go through such agonizing pain over his loss while he was still alive? Nothing made sense. Instead of jumping inside the van to feel and make sure his father was real, Mason shook his head in disbelief and took three steps back.

"Mason, don't," he heard Layla say while she gripped his hand tighter.

But his eyes were focused on the man in front of him with older, yet similar features. Though alive, he looked like he'd been through hell. Dark circles under his eyes. A weak smile on his face. Nothing like the man he saw before he left the fundraising event that dreadful night.

"Son," his father finally spoke. His voice was weak, almost foreign to Mason's ears. He waved him toward the van. "Come inside so that we can explain everything."

Agent Williams spoke up. "There's a lot you don't know, Mason, and now is the time for us to help fill in some of the blanks for you."

Mason shook his head. "What in the…" His head pounded from the crease in his forehead.

"I know this seems unreal, but this had to be done in order to finally take down The Gathering. There was no other way," Agent Williams tried to explain.

He cast pleading eyes toward Layla, but she stepped closer to Mason and squeezed his hand in reassurance again. "Mason, it's up to you. We can go home or follow them." She looked at Agent Williams again. "We are not getting in that van. The president of the

United States could be inside, I don't care. Is there somewhere else we can meet you?" She looked at Mason. "Maybe later?"

The tension among the group was thicker than the soles of his combat boots, and everyone looked at him to make the next move. But he couldn't move, at least not in the way they were probably expecting. So many emotions rippled through his core. Confusion. Relief. Anger. Disappointment. And a tiny bit of admiration.

Agent Williams hesitated like he knew or hoped Mason would change his mind. He looked between Mason and his father and finally relented. "Well, it's been a long night, and we could all use a little time to process what's happening." And by *we,* he knew the agent was referring to him, and he'd be right. Mason seemed to be the only person confused and shocked about the ordeal. "Ms. Langston, do you mind if I send you the address?"

"No, I don't. I have an iPhone, so you can send me a pin to the location."

Layla whipped out her phone to get the contact information and meeting location from Agent Williams. He'd looked at Mason one final time before tapping his arm and climbing into the van. The agent looked between Mason and his father again. Neither of them moved, and Mason had to wonder if his father had free will. Was there a reason he stayed inside? Shouldn't he have come to him to explain what was happening?

"See you tomorrow if you want your questions answered. Eight a.m."

After Agent Williams closed the door with Mason's father still inside the van. Mason and Layla watched the van ease away from the curb, disappearing into the night fog. The last thing he saw was his father's eyes. Was that disappointment like the time his father caught him in a lie about skipping class back in high school? Confusion like the day he told him about his enlisting in the military? Or was he heartbroken because of the pain he knew Mason had gone through over the past several months?

Layla tugged at his hand and gave another comforting squeeze. "C'mon. Let's go back to your place."

He appreciated that she didn't try to sway him one way or the other, but allowed him to navigate his feelings and make his own decision. She'd been with him for the past few months and knew how much he'd give anything to have his father back, yet she didn't push. She understood him, yet another reason he loved her.

Although his hand swallowed hers, Layla's touch was the only thing that brought him comfort and held him together right now. He returned the squeeze. How could he have ever gone through this situation without her?

∞

Layla should be home sleeping in her own bed tonight, but Mason needed her. Seeing his father alive after believing he was dead for the past several months had to be traumatic. And besides, he asked her to stay and offered her his bed while he slept on the reclining sofa, yet she found herself next to him in the spot she occupied earlier.

205

She held his hand while her heart broke into pieces the size of Nerds candy for him. As the events of the evening unfolded, she tried to think about how she'd respond if it were her. But she came up empty. In fact, she probably would have been in such shock that she'd respond in a similar fashion as Mason.

They'd stopped by the store on the way back to his house, and she grabbed a box of peppermint tea bags. She brewed mugs of tea for each of them when they returned to his house. Her mug was half-empty, while he'd only taken one sip. He simply stared ahead at the movie on TV, which had been playing for the last hour.

"I can't believe he's alive. I'm happy about that, but I'm also angry, and a part of me feels bad for feeling this way." His voice was low and thoughtful.

Before she could say anything, he turned to her, looked her in the eye, and added, "I mean, I should be thankful, right?"

"I honestly wish I had all the answers for you because I don't like seeing you this way. But I can't tell you how you should feel. Your feelings are valid, and you have a right to them."

"Did you know?"

Layla couldn't believe he'd ask her something like that or believe she would have that kind of information and withhold it from him.

"Of course, I didn't know your father was still alive."

"What about your dreams? Did you ever have a dream alluding to the fact he may still be alive?"

"No, Mason. I wouldn't keep that from you knowing how you were grieving for him. I care about you too much."

"That's all I need to know." Mason lifted the back of her hand to his lips and planted a soft kiss there. He had no idea the effect he had on her. Maintaining control of her pulse while holding his hand, she'd mastered, but anytime his lips came anywhere near her, her heart decided it would do its own thing, making her feel like it was seconds away from creating another space in her chest. She hid her reaction by filling her lungs with air and releasing it as slow as possible. Mason couldn't know that he drove her crazy, but in a good way. "I care about you, too, Layla, probably way more than I should when we consider how long we've known each other."

"I don't think there's a timeframe to determine when feelings for someone should kick in." She'd said that to convince herself, too, because her emotions were way past logic.

Mason half-smiled for the first time since they'd left his home earlier that evening. "No there isn't, but I have to say thank you for agreeing to stay with me. My mind is just blown right now." He sighed. "We're going to meet them in the morning to get those answers about what has transpired, but I just couldn't do any of that tonight. Thank you for understanding without me having to say anything. That meant a lot to me."

She'd never known Mason to open up so much. The evening's events put him in a vulnerable position.

"You don't have to thank me, but you're welcome. Why don't you drink some of your tea and get some rest?"

"Oh, that's nasty."

Layla burst into laughter, and Mason joined her. "You're not much of a tea drinker, are you?"

"That was your way of comforting me, so I wasn't going to stop you. All I wanted was for you to be here with me. I didn't need anything or anyone else."

Layla's chest swelled.

Swelled from Mason's words.

Swelled from the uncontrollable thumping of her heart.

Before long, he'd have her professing her love for him if she wasn't careful.

"You're very sweet. Thank you."

"I mean it, Layla." Mason straightened his posture and turned toward her. "I don't want you to think I'm telling you this because I'm in some emotionally weird place, because I'm certain about my feelings for you, no matter what's happening. I've never felt this way about any other woman. Layla, I love you."

Mason rubbed her chin, drawing her lips closer to his. And whether he was acting out of his disheveled feelings or not, in this moment, she didn't really care. She succumbed to the familiar feeling of melting whenever his lips touched hers, and this moment was no different. As she drew closer to him, that console in between them blocked her movement, reminding her to stay in the safe zone.

Layla broke the kiss. She rubbed the back of his neck and maintained eye contact. Looking at him, she could see that what he said was true and that her feelings were reciprocated. His eyes made her comfortable enough to share her own truth. "I love you, too, Mason."

CHAPTER TWENTY-TWO

Mason held Layla's hand as they walked to his truck that morning. Now that they'd professed their love for each other, he wondered how they would move forward after she finished this story and no longer needed a mentor. They'd stayed up until two o'clock in the morning talking about everything except where their relationship would go from this point. Well, they hadn't even established that they would be in a committed relationship. And that made him crazy, too.

But he also needed to see this story through to the end first.

He drove to the address Agent Williams gave Layla last night, which was a little blue house in a quaint neighborhood in Sealy, Texas. The next house was about an eighth of a mile down the road. For the most part, Mason and Layla had seen fields with cows and horses as they drew closer to their destination. It was quiet in the area. In fact, they hadn't seen any cars pass by since they took the exit off Interstate 10.

A man dressed in a white buttoned-down shirt and dark gray slacks stood on the porch with his hands crossed in front of him. His only company was a white porch swing. With his serious, no-nonsense expression, Mason assumed he was also an FBI agent.

He couldn't believe any of this was real.

He unbuckled his seatbelt and took a deep breath. "Ready?"

Layla nodded. "There's no time like the present." She grabbed his wrist before he moved to get out of the truck. "Hey, everything is going to be okay. No matter what we find out in there, try to look at the big picture."

And by big picture, she meant that his father was still alive.

"I'll try," he said. Because that was all he could do.

So many emotions bottled up inside of him threatening to unleash at any given moment.

So many unknowns.

So many questions.

He climbed out of the vehicle and rounded the rear to open the door for Layla. She took him by surprise when she grabbed his hand for support. Before today, she'd always shown her affection privately, but in this case, he was glad she'd broken the rules.

Mason's chest felt equally as heavy as his feet when he climbed the steps. The fact that his father was still alive should have brought him joy, and there was a part of him that celebrated, but a deeper part of him needed answers. How could the man he'd loved and who'd loved him all his life keep such a secret from him?

He and Layla hadn't fully ascended the six steps leading to the porch when Agent Williams came out of the front door. "Glad you two made it. Come on inside."

The agent who stood watch didn't speak, only nodded his agreement that it was okay for them to enter. No doubt he knew who they were and why they'd come.

Mason released Layla's hand. Under any other circumstance, he would have allowed her to enter first, but he couldn't do so right now, not knowing who or what was inside. Agent Williams still hadn't gained his trust. As soon as he stepped foot inside the house, he scanned the area. The home was small. The living room connected to the kitchen. Simple furnishings. One sofa. Two chairs. A coffee table. A flat-screen TV hung on the otherwise plain white walls. Probably two bedrooms and bathrooms.

Agent Williams skirted around him. "Please have a seat."

When he and Layla sat, his father entered the room with a limp he didn't have before. He looked tired and worn out as if he hadn't slept in days. Mason's breath caught in his chest. And while his anger still simmered beneath the surface, he had to lay hands on his father to ensure he wasn't a figment of his imagination.

Mason leaped out of his seat and gripped his father in a bear hug. His weak arms encircled Mason as well. His eyes grew wet, so he had to let his father go. Taking a few steps back, he assessed his father's apologetic eyes. Whatever happened since the explosion had taken a toll on him. He gestured for Mason to sit on the sofa with Layla while he sat in the nearest rocking recliner chair.

Hunching forward with his elbows on his knees and his hands clasped, he waited for his father or Agent Williams to speak. When the room was quiet for seconds too long, Mason said, with his attention focused on his father, "So tell me what's going on. Why have I been grieving my father, yet he's sitting right in front of me?"

Agent Williams cleared his throat. "First, let me apologize to you, Mr. Sterling. Walter has been working with us for quite some time while we gathered evidence against the individuals involved in The Gathering. Thankfully, your father wasn't close enough to the impact point of the explosion to sustain deadly injuries—"

Mason interjected. "But I identified his body. I buried him."

"Well, yes and no. We gave him a drug that lowered his heartbeat, making it undetectable. We had to go through the motions of the funeral, and we couldn't tell you because we had to make it look real."

Mason's voice rose. "So you'd prefer to have me grieve my father? In what world does that make sense?" He turned to his father. "And how could you approve of this?"

"He didn't know. For a month, he was in a medically induced coma to help him heal from the injuries he sustained from the explosion. I hope you can understand that we were trying to protect him so that the person responsible for the explosion, whom we now know was Donovan Finch, wouldn't come after him again. And once The Gathering made the mistake of killing Detective Mansfield, we knew it wouldn't be long before we caught them. We just needed time to gather the evidence."

"I'm sorry, son. I couldn't tell you that I'd started working with the FBI over a year ago. They contacted me right after I launched my campaign. Shortly after, Donovan approached me, as well as a few others, about helping The Gathering secure funding for a real estate venture. The Gathering promised support if I continued helping them the same as Congresswoman Lackey had done in the past."

"This is insane."

"I know it's a lot to make sense of right now, but it's over. Those folks are going to jail, and I'm going home."

Agent Williams inserted himself into the conversation. "That's right. We'll hold a press conference and give a high-level overview of what happened and how the situation is under control. Walter is free to live his normal life now."

"Except it isn't normal. Did either of you stop to think about how this will affect his life going forward?"

"Everything will be fine, Mason. I've done my civic duty, and now I can live the rest of my retired days out in peace. I'm okay with my new life going forward."

Every muscle in his body seized. His chest was wrecked with pain. This situation was unreal, putting him at a loss for words, something he'd hardly ever say about himself.

Mason rested his head against his steepled fingers, trying to process everything he'd just heard. Why wasn't his father as bothered by the outcome of this situation as him? Their lives were forever changed.

∞

Layla placed a gentle hand on Mason's tense shoulder. This had to be a lot for him to take in because it was plenty for her, and it wasn't her father sitting before them who was believed to be dead, but now alive.

When Mason looked like he needed time to process, she jumped in with her own questions. "I'm curious: Why did Mr. Sterling come along with you when you arrested The Gathering?"

"We knew you two would be there, and if things got out of hand, we believed that Mason seeing Walter alive would prevent him from doing anything he couldn't take back."

"How'd you know we'd be there?"

Agent Williams readily admitted, "We've been watching you. I knew that Mason would stop at nothing to get the answers he sought, but I couldn't intervene and tell him the truth about his father, and I also had to ensure that you two didn't interfere with our investigation."

"What you mean is that you've been following us," Layla corrected.

She didn't know if she should be thankful because that meant the FBI was protecting them or feeling violated.

Agent Williams shrugged. His behavior was nonchalant, and she didn't like it.

"Where were you all when our vehicles were vandalized?"

"We were surveilling you, not your vehicles."

Well, in her mind, she couldn't be sure how good they were at their jobs. If the FBI was watching her, they should be protecting everything—her person and her property. She refrained from rolling her eyes.

"And the files? Why did Detective Mansfield have the files? What did she have to do with any of this?"

"She was part of the joint task force with the FBI—a valuable member of our team. We are all sadden by her loss of life, but we're encouraged because it was her work that helped us find the members of The Gathering."

Layla was halfway satisfied with his response. Shouldn't his team have protected her, too?

"So, is Mr. Sterling free to go home? And are we free to publish our story?" Before he could answer, she continued. "Initially we were investigating Congresswoman Lackey and her political misconduct and possible covering up of her son's murder of Flex Technology's COO, which we've now learned that Donovan Finch was behind as well. This information about The Gathering has exposed an entire organization of political corruption." She glanced at Mason because she hoped it wasn't too soon to bring up the reason she was there in the first place. This would be her first big story contribution—her chance to prove herself.

Mason looked at her then back at Agent Williams. "You're not planning to try and censor us, are you?"

"As long as your story is fact, no. However, our office will need to review it before it's published to ensure no classified information is revealed."

"And just how would we have anything classified?" Mason asked the question before Layla could get the words out of her mouth.

"Just precaution. I do hope you understand."

She didn't, but whatever.

Mason stood and stuffed his hands in his pockets. He'd obviously had enough of this conversation. "I see no reason why we need to remain here any longer. Dad, are you ready?"

Mr. Sterling stood as if it pained him to do so. "I am. I'm ready to go home."

"What would you have done if I'd sold your house?"

Mr. Sterling chuckled. "I guess I'd be living with you."

And for the first time since arriving, Mason laughed.

CHAPTER TWENTY-THREE

Two weeks later, Mason and Layla sat in Simon's office discussing their story exposing The Gathering—the result of their investigation into Congresswoman Lackey and her family. What began as a story about Congresswoman Lackey and her son morphed into something much bigger—and that was yet another thing he loved about his work. They'd uncovered political corruption and exposed murderers.

Time helped him heal and process the events since the explosion. And while he didn't agree with the FBI's methods, he wasn't as angry today as he was when he discovered he'd been lied to. He had Layla to thank for the change in perspective.

Simon leaned back in his chair and linked his hands over his belly. "You alright, man? You've been through quite the hell storm."

He cast a quick glance at Layla before turning his attention to Simon. "I'm about as good as can be expected. Finding out my dad is still alive, no matter how insane the whole thing is, is a good deal."

"Right. And Chief Gritlock even called you to offer his apologies. I didn't think the man knew how to apologize, especially not to you."

The three of them shared a laugh.

"Trust me, I'll probably never hear those words from him again. I should've recorded him. The fact that he knew my father was still alive explains why he acted the way he did when we went to pay him a visit. He's never been a fan of mine, but he was different that day. Now I know why. You didn't know about my father, did you?"

Mason didn't think it was true, but he had to ask. As part of the joint task force, Detective Mansfield knew before she was killed. Chief Gritlock also knew. Mason had to wonder who else had been briefed other than him.

"Nah, man. I couldn't have done that to you. I'm glad he's alive, and it's worth saying that I hope you know the opportunity you have. Cherish these moments with your old man."

"No doubt." Mason paused a beat before asking, "So was our buddy at the FBI okay with the story?"

Even mentioning his work in the same sentence as the FBI in this regard was insane.

Simon waved him off. "Yeah, he was fine. He knew you didn't have any classified information. Where would you have gotten it in the first place? He just wanted to throw his weight around a little. I was never worried about him."

"I figured as much, but I don't want any trouble with any organizations that have three-letter acronyms."

"That goes for both of us." There was a gleam in Simon's eye, which let Mason know he probably wouldn't agree with whatever he was about to say next. "I hate to put you on the spot in front of Layla, but how did it feel to be a mentor?" He pointed toward his laptop screen. "I'm going to go out on a limb and say you loved it because this is probably some of the best work that I've ever seen from you."

The trio burst into laughter again.

"That's because Layla wrote the piece. It would've been a conflict of interest for me to write the story considering the situation with my dad."

"I agree."

"Let's also agree that putting me on the spot is definitely your thing, but to answer your question…" He paused and cast another glance at Layla's smiling face before he returned his attention to Simon. "I didn't want to be a mentor at first, and you know that. I do my best work alone—at least that's what I thought before Layla. It was cool having a someone to talk through theories with, but it couldn't have been just anyone. You made a good choice. She'll be just fine on her own from here on out."

His chest pained with his last words. He didn't want Layla to be on her own any more than he wanted to poke himself in the eye with his pencil, but he knew this day was coming.

"Of course, she will. That's why I hired her. I can spot talent, and this piece right here," he said, pointing at his laptop again, "is gold. You two are an amazing combination. And Mason, you've gone far by yourself, but I hope this experience showed you that you can go even further playing well with others."

As Simon's friend, Mason knew he wanted to say more. Whenever they talked alone, they had no issues speaking on a personal level, but with Layla in the room, Simon held back. He couldn't be sure how much longer that would last. He'd hinted at the fact he sensed things had gotten personal between him and Layla, but he'd never gotten a chance to talk with Simon about it because he'd been busy with the story.

Mason saluted him. "I've learned my lesson, boss."

"Good, because I have a proposition for you, but first I'd like to get some feedback from Layla about her experience here at *The Houston Exposure,* you as her mentor, and whether she wants to continue pursuing a career in journalism."

Mason and Layla had this discussion a couple of times where he'd shared his feelings on the matter, and she did the same. They enjoyed working together, and while they still hadn't defined the parameters of their relationship, he would continue to see her now that she no longer needed him to officially serve as her mentor. And while she'd expressed that she had every intention of sticking with her new career in journalism, he'd feel better to hear her declare the news to Simon.

That would end her probationary period and make her position permanent.

And permanent sounded good to him, not just for the job, but for him and her as well.

∞

When she'd walked into Simon's office four months ago, Mason nearly had a stroke. But she now knew him as caring and compassionate and the man who made her heart pen its own story. And while she loved him, he had to know that her decision to stay or go and her feedback to Simon were all professional and had nothing to do with her feelings for him.

"Simon, I can't thank you enough for the opportunity—for giving me the chance to do something that I've always loved."

"You're welcome, but your accomplishments and accolades spoke for you. After our first talk, I knew you'd be a great fit for *The Houston Exposure*'s staff. Trust me, we needed you here."

Layla's heart swelled with gratitude. She'd set out to do something for herself—to explore and identify Layla outside of Langston Brands—and she'd done just that.

"Thank you, Simon."

He clasped his hands. "Okay, now for the nitty gritty. How did Mason do? Do I need to ask him to leave out so you can speak freely?"

"No, he can stay." She looked at Mason and maintained eye contact with him when she answered Simon's questions. "Mason was great. Patient. He allowed me the opportunity to explore theories, build my investigative skills, and gave me autonomy. He was and is a good teacher. I think he might have earned a raise."

Mason quirked an eyebrow and held a laugh.

"I'm sorry, is this about work or something else? Did he promise you half of his raise if he were to get one?" Simon asked.

Layla put on her best straight face. "Of course not." She cleared her throat. "Seriously, he was and is a great coach. He challenged me, but not only that, I appreciated his professionalism and his openness to my ideas. Although he's been in this career for years, he wasn't arrogant, and him trusting me made the most difference—made me comfortable with my decisions."

"Wow." Simon pointed to Mason. "Are we talking about the same Mason? I should've brought you in here years ago."

Mason and Simon shared a laugh. "Stop that. We don't want her to think she's wrong about how great I am."

Layla enjoyed the banter and camaraderie between the two of them.

"Alright, so does this mean that you'll be staying with us here at *The Houston Exposure* because we'd love to have you permanently. I've been reading Mason's stories for years, and it's clear that there's something special about the one you two just finished. It has your touch—a touch that only Layla Langston can give."

Inside, her heart leaped. She'd done something for herself outside of her family's brand and name. She had no reservations about staying, but a part of her heart was saddened by what staying meant. Staying meant a permanent good-bye to the life she'd established at Langston Brands. That was what she wanted, right?

"Yes, I want to stay."

Mason smiled big, then reached over to pull her into his arms. Currents of electricity sliced through her being. The love and softness in his eyes were clear when he released her. "Welcome aboard, Layla."

Simon reached across the desk to shake her hand. "Thank you for choosing us. All the official paperwork will be in your inbox by the end of day."

"Thank you."

A broader smile framed Simon's face. He clasped his hands as if he had something juicy to tell them. "Well, since you love working together so much, there's a story I think you two would be interested in covering in D.C. Layla, do you want to spend another few months or longer looking at that face?" He pointed to Mason.

D.C.? Her heart lurched in her throat. Sweat beads formed on the back of her neck. She was prepared to stay, but not be so far away from her family for months at a time. Or longer.

Simon squinted. "You look like you need time to think about it. Don't feel obligated to take this assignment. There are plenty of local stories to cover if that's what you'd prefer."

This is what you wanted, remember?

Layla swallowed her fear. "I want to go."

Mason fist bumped her. "That's my girl."

Simon's fingers slid across his laptop's keypad, then he reached into his desk drawer and removed a file. "Here you go."

Mason picked up the file and flipped it open. Layla leaned over and peered inside. "*Ooh,* this is going to be good."

"My thoughts exactly."

EPILOGUE

Layla twirled around so that Crystal and Ava could get a full view of her little black dress on their FaceTime call. Sleeveless with the hem hitting mid-thigh, she felt a little self-conscious. She and Mason had made their relationship official before they started their assignment in D.C. seven months ago. They'd gone out to dinner more times than she could count, so she wasn't sure why the bout of anxiety showed itself tonight.

Ava whistled. "Spicy. You want him to eat you or the steak?"

Crystal and Layla laughed. "You've gotten married, and now you're out of control. That sounds like something I would say."

"I don't know, Layla. Ava is right. You look hot in that dress. Where are y'all going again, and what's the occasion?"

Layla positioned the phone on the hotel's bathroom counter and touched up her makeup. "I appreciate you two boosting my head up."

Crystal chuckled. "No boosting necessary. You are fire. What are you trying to do, make the man put a ring on it?"

They all laughed. "Don't move me too fast, Crys. We're just enjoying our time together. Work has been crazy, so we're going to the Skydome restaurant tonight to unwind with some good food."

"Hold on, let me check it out." A moment later, Ava said, "I don't know, Lay, the Skydome seems pretty romantic. Have you Googled it?"

"Yes, I have. It has a rotating rooftop that I can't wait to see at night."

Crystal and Ava *tsk*ed.

"Well, I'm glad he's treating you well out there. I can tell you're happy because your face is glowing," Crystal said.

Layla paused to assess her reflection in the mirror. It was true. She hadn't stopped smiling since they'd been on the phone— well, all day really.

Ava chimed in. "Right. We miss you in Houston."

Layla grabbed the phone, walked into the suite's sitting area, and sat on the sofa. She held the phone up to her face so that she could see her sisters. "I miss you all, too, but I'm so glad I took a chance on this job. It's been nice to learn something new while getting a chance to pursue a career I've wanted to go after for years. How are things with Langston Brands?"

"Great. We're gearing up for the launch of our new leather collection—Tres Jolie."

Layla smiled, reminiscing about product launch meetings she'd been involved in over the years. "I love the name of the new collection. Ava came up with that, didn't she?"

Crystal laughed. "How'd you guess?"

"Just a hunch."

Ava defended herself. "Hey, it's fitting because we want women to look and feel very pretty when wearing the bags. Hence the name. Are you coming home for the launch party?"

"Yep. Already booked my plane ticket."

"Great. We can't wait to see you. How's the job going in D.C?"

"It's good. No complaints. Mason is still great at mentoring me, although he says I don't need any mentoring."

"And he's right. But if I haven't said it enough, I am proud of you for not being afraid to start over."

"Thanks, Crys."

The truth was that in the beginning she was afraid to start over, only she didn't allow her fear to stop her. And if it wasn't for those dreadful dreams, she may not have moved on the opportunity just yet. As scary as the dreams slash nightmares were, she was thankful that they pushed her out of her comfort zone.

Marcel Jr. whimpered, and Crystal picked him up so that he could also be in the video. "Say hello to Aunt Ava and Aunt Lay." Using a baby voice, she teased Layla about Mason proposing.

Ava laughed, and a sheepish grin spread across her lips. "Speaking of babies," she paused for dramatic effect, and before she could finish her statement, Layla squealed, "You're preggers?"

Ava nodded and sucked her bottom lip between her teeth. "Yes. I took the test last night. We weren't going to say anything until I went to the doctor, but I had to tell you two."

Both Crystal and Layla congratulated her. Even Marcel Jr. grinned.

"I told Zeke this morning," Zack announced in the background.

Ava chuckled and shook her head. "And he said I'd be the first to spill the beans. But please don't tell Mom and Dad. I want to have the sonogram in hand when I deliver the news."

Layla made a zipping motion across her lips, and she and Ava waited for Crystal to agree.

"Why are y'all looking at me like that? I'm not going to say anything."

Ava folded her arms across her chest and hiked an eyebrow. "Somehow I don't believe you."

"Promise."

"Okay. I've gotta run. I'll call later."

"Tonight," Crystal interjected. "I'll be up anyway because of this little guy. We want to know how this romantic dinner goes. Who knows? You may have some news to share of your own."

"It's not a romantic dinner. We're just hanging out. I'm about to get off this FaceTime because y'all are not about to get in my head." And make her even more self-conscious than she already was. Or begin to secretly wish for marriage and babies.

Mason knocked rhythmically on her door. She grabbed her crossbody chain-strapped handbag and slipped it on her shoulder before answering.

"Hey, I'm ready," she announced when she opened the door. Her heart and belly somersaulted at the sight of him in a black suit and crisp white shirt, which was unbuttoned at the neck, exposing his collarbone and showing off his swag.

Mason whistled, reminding her of her sisters' teasing, however, she appreciated his approving scan. "Yes, you are." He pulled her into his arms and squeezed. "How is it possible that you look even more beautiful every time I see you?"

The better question was how was it possible that he made her heart write a new song every time she was in his presence?

∞

After he gave his keys to the valet, he strolled around his truck to help Layla. Hand in hand, they walked inside of the Doubletree hotel and took the elevator to the rooftop restaurant, Skydome. For the past month, he'd researched the perfect restaurant to make this evening memorable for him and Layla. A view of the D.C. skyline in a rotating rooftop restaurant couldn't be more perfect.

Part of him wanted to start and end the evening when she answered the door earlier. Layla was the most beautiful and interesting woman he'd ever met, but more so than that, she was the only one who'd set his soul ablaze.

When they arrived at the hostess station and gave his last name for the reservation, he thought back to his father's advice as he and Layla followed the hostess to their table. *Just love her, and I mean really love her. Wholeheartedly and sacrificially. If you can't do that, then don't ask her to marry you because you aren't ready.* But by the time their conversation ended, his father knew how much he loved Layla and wanted to spend the rest of his life with her.

He was ready.

But he was also nervous.

Layla gasped and directed his attention to the skyline. "Mason, this is beautiful. I've never experienced anything like this back in Houston. How'd you hear about this place?"

"Researched it online. I wanted to take you somewhere nice. You deserve it. All we've done is work on this case, not really taking much time for ourselves. I think it's important that we do that more often. We're only here for a short time, so we need to enjoy it."

Their waitress stopped by to bring glasses of water to their table and announced she'd give them time to look over their menus.

Layla raised her water glass. "I agree. And in the spirit of taking time for ourselves, no talking about work tonight."

Mason lifted his water glass in salute. "I can get with that."

They spent the next few minutes perusing the menu.

"Okay, since I always order salmon, I'm going to live on the edge tonight and order the steak."

Mason chuckled. "The edge, huh? I'll go with the same." The bubbly waitress with shoulder-length braids returned to their table.

"Welcome to Skydome. Have you dined with us before?"

"First timers," Mason said.

Her eyes lit up, clearly excited about the opportunity to talk about the menu and her favorites. After she'd finished and Layla asked her a few questions, they placed their orders for the steaks they'd originally decided they'd order. According to the waitress, they couldn't go wrong with anything on the menu, so Mason felt comfortable in their selection.

When she left, Layla's eyes lit up. "Guess what? I'm going to be an aunt again. I just found out before we left."

"Really? Congrats. Crystal and the DA are going to have another baby?"

Layla shook her head. "No. Ava is pregnant."

"Congrats to her."

And suddenly Mason's entire future flashed before his eyes because he wanted all of that—marriage and kids—with Layla. Of all the things they'd discussed, the topic of kids had never come up.

"And what about you? Do you want children?"

Layla was hesitant, though he couldn't understand why. She released a sigh. "I do, but I'm now forty, and I'm not married yet, so not sure if it'll happen for me. If it doesn't, I'm okay with being an aunt. Sure, I can adopt, but I don't want to raise children alone. We were a handful for my parents, so I wouldn't choose to parent alone. What about you?"

"Absolutely. I've always had a great relationship with my father, and it would be an honor for me to carry on the Sterling name. Three kids would be ideal, but I'm okay with whatever number God blesses me with."

Layla offered a smile that made him believe she was pleased with his response, and that could've been all in his head given that all he could think about right now was spending the rest of his life with her.

And while his plan was to wait until dessert, he could no longer hold back. The moment was right.

"I know we said we wouldn't bring up work, but remember the night you said you were workshopping a team name for us?"

Layla bubbled in laughter. "Yeah, I do. I also remember you looking at me like I was crazy."

Mason chuckled. "What did you come up with?"

"Nothing yet. If you need me to get back on that, I will," she sang.

"I have one."

"You do? Let's hear it."

He locked gazes with her. His heart leaped every time a moment like that passed between them. "What about Team Sterling?"

"Team Sterling? Is that all you came up with?"

Mason waited for a moment to allow his words to sink in. After a few seconds, recognition and tears filled her eyes. "Mason," she whispered.

He pushed away from the table, kneeled on one knee, and removed the small velvet box from his jacket. "Layla Langston, I love you with every fiber of my being, and I don't want to go through the rest of my life without you as my wife. Will you marry me?"

Layla bobbed her head up and down and held out her left hand. "Yes. I'll marry you."

She got up and sat on his bended knee. Mason slipped the ring on her finger. She wrapped her arms around his head and kissed him until they were both breathless.

Layla used her thumb to rub her red lipstick off his lips. "Team Sterling it is."

Dear reader,

What did you think of Layla and Mason? I adored the two of them together. And who knows? Maybe they'll have their own series one day. We can never be too sure.

In the story, Mason had to work through his grief, while Layla was on an exploration to live life on purpose. How many of us want to live the life God has predestined for us, yet we're afraid to make changes because we feel like it is too late? Maybe we allow age, resources, or circumstances to hold us back.

But, like Layla, I don't think it's ever too late to begin again. As long as you have breath in your body and you feel that nudge from the Holy Spirit to take a leap, take it! And when you do, I'd love to hear about it.

And like Mason, if you're experiencing grief, my prayer is that God wraps you in His love and comfort and place people in your path to help you through it. Hugs to you.

I hope you enjoyed The Missing Link. Please take a moment to let me know what you think by leaving a review on Amazon/Goodreads/Bookbub.

Until next time,
Natasha

About the Author

Natasha fell in love with love around the age of twelve because of artists like Babyface, Boys II Men, Whitney Houston, and New Edition. Around sixteen when her mother purchased a romance novel and left it lying around the house untouched, Natasha read it and a spark for the written word had been ignited.

Natasha believes that writing is one of her purposes and contributions to the world. She feels accomplished when she can get a few words written and like blah when life gets in the way. Her hope is that at the end of every novel, readers will feel like they've been wrapped in a cozy blanket with a mug of their favorite coffee/tea/warm drink.

When she isn't reading or writing, she is likely working out or watching movies with her family. Natasha resides in Richmond, TX with her husband, Eddie Frazier, Jr. and their three children, Eden, Ethan, and Emilyn. Her greatest joy and commitment is to her family who she hopes to inspire above all else. One of her many mottos in life is: Faith removes limitations. Natasha and her family attend Parkway Fellowship in Richmond, TX, where she volunteers as an Usher. Natasha is also a member of the Houston Area Alumni Chapter of Jackson State University and Alpha Kappa Alpha Sorority, Inc.

Connect with Natasha online:

Bookbub @NatashaDFrazier
Instagram @author_natashafrazier

Twitter or X @author_natashaf
TikTok @author_natashafrazier
Facebook @craves.2012
Website: www.natashafrazier.com

Also by Natasha D. Frazier

Devotionals

The Life Your Spirit Craves

Not Without You

Not Without You Prayer Journal

The Life Your Spirit Craves for Mommies

Pursuit

Fiction

Love, Lies & Consequences

Through Thick & Thin: Love, Lies & Consequences Book 2

Shattered Vows: Love, Lies & Consequences Book 3

Out of the Shadows: Love, Lies & Consequences Book 4

Kairos: The Perfect Time for Love

Fate (The Perfect Time for Love series)

With Every Breath (The McCall Family Series, book 1)

With Every Step (The McCall Family Series, book 2)

With Every Moment (The McCall Family Series, book 3)

The Reunion (Langston Sisters, book1)

The Wrong Seat (Langston Sisters, book 2)

Non-Fiction

How Long Are You Going to Wait?

Milton Keynes UK
Ingram Content Group UK Ltd.
UKHW012243291123
433483UK00001B/164